There was a warning signal

Rock threw the door open and went in with a rush. A gun blasted from the darkness and a bullet snatched at his jacket. He pressed himself against the wall, his hand hard on his gun.

There was a dart of light from the fireplace and he caught a glimpse of Sharon, her eyes wide with fright.

Suddenly Zapata lunged from the shadows, his face a snarl of bared teeth and gleaming eyes.

Rock's gun barked and Zapata staggered back, firing wildly. He spun around and plunged through the sack-covered window.

Rock ran to the opening and raised his gun. A ragged streak of lightning tore through the sky, and he could see the front of the half-breed's shirt darkening with pounding rain and with blood.

Rock lowered his gun and turned to Sharon.

"Run," she cried. "They'll kill you if they find you here!"

Fawcett Gold Medal Books
by Louis L'Amour:

The Tall Stranger

by Louis L'Amour

FAWCETT GOLD MEDAL • NEW YORK

Copyright © 1957 CBS Publications, The Consumer Publishing Division of CBS, Inc.

Published by Fawcett Gold Medal Books, a unit of CBS Publications, the Educational and Professional Publishing Division of CBS, Inc.

All rights reserved under International and Pan-American Copyright Conventions. Published in the United States by Ballantine Books, a division of Random House, Inc., New York, and simultaneously in Canada by Random House of Canada Limited, Toronto.

All characters in this book are fictional and any resemblance to persons living or dead is purely coincidental.

ISBN 0-449-14218-3

Printed in the United States of America

First Fawcett Gold Medal Edition: October 1957
First Ballantine Books Edition: December 1983
First Canadian Edition: August 1983

I

WITH SLOW, ponderously rhythmical steps the oxen moved, each step a pause and an effort, each movement a deadening drag. Fine white dust hung in a sifting cloud above the wagon train, caking the nostrils of animals and men, blanketing the sides of oxen and horses, dusting a thin film over men and women. And the miles stretched on before them, endless and timeless.

Red-rimmed and bloodshot eyes stared with dazed weariness into that limitless distance before them, seeing nothing to grip the eye or hold the attention. Long since all had been forgotten but the heat, the dust and the aching muscles. Each step lifted a powdery dust, stifling and irritating. It lay a foot deep on the plain, drowning the sparse grass and sage.

Rock Bannon, riding away from the train alone, drew in his steel-dust stallion and turned in the saddle, glancing back at the covered wagons, sixteen of them in the long line with some led horses and a few outriders, yet none who rode so far out as himself, and none who appreciated their problems as thoroughly as he did himself.

From where he sat he could not see their faces, but in the days just past he had seen them many times, and the expression of each was engraved in his mind. Haggard, worn, hungry for rest and cool water, he knew that in the heart of each there was a longing to stop.

The vision was in them yet, the golden promise of the distant hills, offering a land of milk and honey, the fair and flowering land sought by all wandering peoples of whatever time or place. No hardship could seem too great, no trail too long, no mountain impassable when the vision was upon them.

It was always and forever the same when men saw the future opening beyond the hills where the sun slept, yet this time the vision must hold meaning; this time the end of the trail must bring realization—for they had brought their women and children along.

All but Rock Bannon. He had neither woman nor child, nor anyone anywhere. He had a horse and a saddle, a ready gun and a mind filled with lore of the trail, and eyes ever fixed on something he wanted, something faint and indistinct in outline, ever distant, yet ever real. Only of late, as he rode alone on the far flank of the wagon train, had that something begun to take shape and outline, and the shape was that of Sharon Crockett.

His somber green eyes slanted back now to the last wagon but one, where the red-gold hair of Sharon on the driver's seat was a flame no dust could dim. In the back of that heavily loaded wagon was Tom Crockett, her father, restless with fever and hurt, nursing a bullet wound in his thigh, a memento of the battle with Buffalo Hide's warriors.

From the head of the train came a long, melodious halloo. Cap Mulholland swung his arm in a great circle, and the lead oxen turned ponderously to swing in the beginning of the circle. Rock touched the gray with his heels and rode slowly toward the wagon train. He was never sure these days as to his reception.

Cap's beard was white with dust as he looked up. Weariness and worry showed in his face. "Rock," he said, "we could sure use a little fresh meat. We're all a mite short on rations, and you seem to be the best hunter among us."

"All right," Rock said. "I'll see what I can do after I get Crockett's wagon in place."

Mulholland's head turned sharply. "Bannon, I'd let that girl alone if I were you. No offense intended, but she ain't your kind. I ain't denyin' you've been a sight of help to us. In fact, I don't know what we'd have done without you, and we're glad you came along. But Sharon Crockett's another story. Her pa's bedded down now, and in no shape to speak."

Bannon turned the steel dust sharply. His face was grim and his jaw hard. "Did he ask you to speak to me? Or did she?"

"Well, no—not exactly," Mulholland said uncomfortably. "But I'm headin' this train."

"Then I'll thank you to mind your own business. Headin' this wagon train is job enough for any man. Any time the Crocketts ask me to stay away, I'll stay, but that's their affair."

Mulholland's face flushed and his eyes darkened with anger. "She ain't your kind," he persisted, "you bein' a killer, and all."

Rock Bannon stared at him. "You didn't seem to mind my killing Indians!" he said sarcastically. "In fact, you killed a few yourself!"

"Don't get me wrong!" Cap persisted. "I ain't denyin' you helped us! Without you I don't know whether we could have beat off those Indians or not, but killin' Indians and killin' white men's a different thing!"

"You're new to the West, Cap." Bannon's voice was rough. "In a short time you'll find there's white men out here that need killin' a sight worse than Indians. In fact, I'm not so sure those Indians jumped us without help!"

"What do you mean?" Mulholland demanded.

"I mean," Bannon said, "that Morton Harper told you there'd be no hostile Indians on this route! I warned you of Buffalo Hide then, but he told you he ranged further north. You took his advice on this trail, not mine!"

Pagones and Pike Purcell were coming up to join them. Pike heard the last remark and his lean, lantern-jawed face flushed with anger.

"You ridin' Harper again?" he harshly demanded of Bannon. "He said this was a better trail, and it is. We ain't had no high passes, and we had six days of the best travel we've had since we left Council Bluffs, with plenty of water and plenty of grass. Now we get a few bad days and a brush with Indians, but that ain't too much!" He glared at Rock. "I'm sick of your whinin' about this trail and Harper! I figure he's a darned good man. He was sure a help to me when I needed it. Out of supplies and no medicine for the wife, and he staked me."

"I wasn't talking to you," Rock replied shortly, "and I don't like your tone. As far as your loan from Harper, remember that you haven't heard from him on it yet. I've a hunch he'll collect, and plenty!"

"I don't need no killer to tell me my business!" Pike snapped, reining his horse around to face Rock. "And I ain't afraid of a reputation for killin', neither. You don't bluff me none."

"Here, here!" Cap protested. "We can't afford to have trouble in camp. You'll have to admit, Pike, that we'd have been in bad shape a couple of times in that fight, if it hadn't been for Bannon. He's been a help. I don't agree with him on Mort Harper, either, but every man to his own idea."

Rock swung the gray and cantered off toward the hills. Inwardly, he was seething. He was a fool to stay on with the wagon train—he understood that perfectly well. Not a man here liked him, not a man here talked to him except on business. He was not even a member of their train, except by accident.

They had found him at the crossing of the Platte. Riding, half dead, with two bullet wounds in his body, his horse ready to drop with fatigue, he had run upon the wagon train. Sharon Crockett had bedded him down in her wagon and cared for him, and he had ridden on in the same place where her father rode now.

He had offered no explanation of his wounds, and had talked but little. A grim and lonely man, gentle words came hard and he could only look up into Sharon's face and wonder at her beauty, tongue-tied and helpless. Yet his hard, tough, trail-battered body was too used to pain to remain helpless for long. He recovered rapidly, and after that he had ridden along with wagons, hunting for fresh meat and helping when he could.

He was not a man who made friends easily, yet gradually the ice was melting, and the clannishness of the wagon train was breaking down. Twice he had even talked with Sharon, riding beside her wagon, speaking of the mountains and his own wild and lonely life. All that ended abruptly that night beside the campfire at the fort.

They had been seated around the fire eating supper, listening to the bustle of life around the fort, when a tall, handsome man rode up on a beautiful black mare.

Perfectly groomed, his wide white hat topping coal-black hair that hung to his shoulders, a drooping black mustache and a black broadcloth suit, the trousers tucked into hand-tooled boots, Morton Harper had been a picture to take any eye.

Swinging down, he had walked up to the fire. "Howdy, folks!" His voice was genial, his manner warm and pleasant. In an instant his personality and voice had done what Rock Bannon's could not do in two weeks. He had broken down their reserve and become one of the group. "Headin' for California?"

"Reckon we are," Mulholland had agreed. "We ain't rightly decided whether to stay on the Humboldt Trail or to swing north and go to Oregon."

"Why go either way?" Harper asked. "There's a southern route I could recommend that would be much easier going for your womenfolks." His alert eyes had already found and appraised Sharon Crockett. "More water, plenty of grass, and no high mountain passes."

Cap Mulholland looked up with interest. "We ain't heard of no such pass, nor no such trail," he admitted. "How does she go?"

"Man named Hastings scouted some of it, and I scouted the rest myself. It is a more southerly route, and within another few months all the travel will be going that way. Right now," he winked, "the trains that go that way are going to have a mighty fine trip of it. Very little dust except in one stretch, fine grass, lots of water. Also, the hostile Indians are all raiding far north of there along the traveled routes.

"But," he added, "I can see you're well led, and you'll no doubt learn about this trail yourselves. From the look of your teams I'd say you were lucky in your choice of a leader."

Leaning against the hub of a wagon wheel, Rock Bannon ate in silence. The even, smooth flow of the stranger's language had an enchanting quality, but his own hard-grained, cynical character was impervious to mere talk.

As the hours flowed by, Harper sat among them, pleasing the men with subtle flattery, the women with smiles. The reserve of the group thawed under his easy manner, and before long they began to discuss his trail and its possibilities, considering themselves fortunate to know of it first.

There was some talk of putting it to a vote, but it was morning before it came to that. Until then Rock was silent. "You'd do better," he interposed suddenly, "to stick to the regular trail."

Harper's head came up sharply and his eyes leveled at Bannon. "Have you ever been over the trail I suggest, my friend?"

"Part way," Rock replied. "Only part of it."

"And was that part easy going for oxen and horses? Was there a good trail? Grass? Water?"

"Yes, I reckon it has all that, but I still wouldn't advise it."

"You say it is a better trail but you wouldn't advise it." Harper glanced around at the others, smiling tolerantly. "That doesn't make much sense, does it? I've been over the entire trail and found it very good going. Moreover, I can give you a map of the trail showing the water holes, everything. Of course, it's nothing to me what route you take, but if you want to avoid Indians—" He shrugged.

"What about Buffalo Hide?"

Morton Harper's face tightened and his eyes strained to pry Rock Bannon's face from the shadows in which he sat. "He's a Blackfoot. He ranges further north."

Harper's eyes shifted to Mulholland. "Who is this man? I'm surprised he should ask about Buffalo Hide, as he isn't known to most white men, other than renegades. I can't understand why he should try to persuade you to neglect an easier route for a more dangerous one. Is he one of your regular train?"

Pike Purcell was abrupt. From the first day he had disliked and been suspicious of Bannon. "No, he ain't none of our crowd, just a man who tied up with us back yonder a ways. He ain't got no wagon, nothin' but the horse he's ridin'."

"I see." Morton Harper's face became grave with implied doubt. "No offense, friend, but would you mind telling me your name? I know most of the men along this trail, and Colonel Warren was asking about some of them only tonight. You'll admit it is safer to be careful, for there are so many renegades who work with the Indians."

"My name's Rock Bannon."

Morton Harper's lips tightened and his eyes grew wary. For a moment he seemed taken aback. Then, as he perceived where his own interests lay, his eyes lighted with triumph.

"Ah? Bannon, eh? I've heard of you. Killed a man in Laramie a month or so back, didn't you?"

"He drew on me."

Rock was acutely conscious of the sudden chill in the atmosphere, and he could see Sharon's shocked gaze directed at him. The people of the wagon train were fresh from the East. Only Cap had been as far West as the Platte before, and he only once. They were peace-loving men, quiet, and asking no trouble.

Morton Harper was quick to sense his advantage. "Sorry to have brought it up, Bannon," he said smoothly, "but when a man advises a wagon train against their best interests, it is well to inquire the source of the advice."

Bannon got up. He was a tall man, lean-hipped and broad-shouldered, his flat-brimmed hat shadowing his face, his eyes glowing with piercing light as he spoke.

"I still say that route's a fool way to go. This ain't no country to go wanderin' around in, and that route lies through Hardy Bishop's country. You spoke of Hastings. He was the man who advised the Donner Party."

As his footsteps died away in the darkness, the members of the wagon train sat very still, their enthusiasm suddenly dampened by that ill-fated name. They all knew the story. The horror of it still blanketed the trail with its bloody shadow of the party caught by snows in the high passes and starving until they resorted to cannibalism as a way out.

Morton Harper shrugged. "Of course they started on Hastings' trail, but left it too soon, and the route I suggest avoids all the higher passes." His eyes swung around the group, gathering their attention like the reins of a six-horse team, and he led them on with promises and suggestions, an easy flow of calm, quiet talk, stilling their fears, quieting their doubts, offering them grass and water instead of dust and desert.

In the morning, when they moved out, they took the trail Harper had advised, turning off an hour after they left the fort. He glanced back, and smiled when he saw that he was unobserved. Then he wished them luck, promised to overtake them when a message came for which he waited, and galloped back to the fort.

Rock Bannon was with them. He rode close to Sharon's wagon, and after a time she looked up. He had watched her the night before, had seen her fascinated eyes on Harper's face.

"You don't approve, do you?"

He shook his head. Then he smiled, somewhat grimly. He was a dark, good-looking man with a tinge of recklessness in his green eyes.

"My views aren't important," he said, "I don't belong."

"Pike shouldn't have said that," she said. "He's a strange man. A good man, but stubborn and suspicious."

"Not suspicious of the right folks, maybe." -

Her eyes flashed. "You mean Mr. Harper? Why should we be suspicious of him? He was only trying to help."

"I wonder."

"I think," Sharon said sharply, "you'd do better to be a little less suspicious yourself! You admitted this was a good trail!"

"You haven't met Hardy Bishop yet. Nor Buffalo Hide."

"Mr. Harper said that Indian was farther north." She looked at him. "Who is Hardy Bishop? You mentioned him before."

"He's a man who is trying to run cattle at Indian Writing. They say he's insane to try it, but he's claimed seventy miles of range, and he has cattle there. We have to cross his range."

"What's wrong with that?"

"If you cross it, maybe nothing, but Bishop's a funny man. He doesn't like strangers very much. He's going to wonder why you're so far south. He's going to be suspicious."

"Well, let him be suspicious, then!" Sharon said, her eyes bright and her chin lifting. "We don't care, and we won't bother him any. Does he think he owns the whole country?"

"Uh-huh," Rock said, "I'm afraid he does—with some reason, as far as that valley goes. He made it what it is today."

"How could any man make a valley?" Sharon protested. "This is all free country. Anyway, we're just going through."

The conversation had dwindled and died and after a while he rode off to the far flank of the wagon train. Sharon's manner was distinctly stiff, and he could see she was remembering that story of the killing in Laramie. After a few rebuffs he avoided her. Nobody talked to him. He rode alone and camped alone.

II

IT HAD REMAINED like that for six days. They were six days during which Morton Harper's name became one to conjure with. The long green valley down which they moved was unrutted by wagon trains, the grass was green and waving, and water was plentiful. Harper's map showed an accurate knowledge of the country, and was a great help. On the sixth day after leaving the fort, the Indians hit them.

The attack came at daybreak. Rock Bannon, camping near a spring half a mile from the wagons, awoke with a start. It was scarcely light, yet he felt uneasy. Getting to his knees, he saw the steel-dust staring, ears pricked, at a distant pile of rocks. Then he noticed the movement.

Swiftly and silently he saddled the stallion, bridled it and stowed his gear in the saddlebags. Then, rifle in hand, he skirted the trees along the tiny stream and headed back for the wagons. He rode up, and the man on guard got up, stretching. It was the short, heavy-set Pagones. A good man, and a sharp one. He smiled at Bannon.

"Guess Harper had it more right than you when he said there were no hostiles here," he said. "Ain't that right?"

"No," Bannon said sharply. "Get everybody up and ready. We'll be attacked within a few minutes!"

Pagones stared. "Are you crazy?"

"Get busy, man!" Bannon snapped at Pagones. He wheeled and, running from wagon to wagon, slapped the canvas and said, "On your feet! Indians!"

Men boiled from the wagons, crawling into their clothes and grabbing at rifles. "Get around the whole circle!" he told them. "They're in those rocks and a draw that runs along south of us."

Mulholland rushed out and halted, glaring around.

15

The sky was gray in the east and everything lay in a vague, indistinct light. Not a movement showed in the dark width of the prairie. He started for Bannon to protest, when he heard a startled explanation. Wheeling, he saw a long line of red horsemen not over two hundred yards away and coming at a dead run.

Even as his eyes touched them, the nearest Indian broke into a wild, shrill whoop. Then the whole charging line broke into yells.

Rock Bannon, leaning against the Crockett wagon, lifted his Henry rifle and fired. A horse stumbled and went down. He fired again, and an Indian threw up his arms and vanished in the turmoil of oncoming horses and men, and then the men of the wagon train opened up.

Firing steadily, Bannon emptied his rifle before the Indians reached the edge of the circle. One brave, his wild-eyed horse at a dead run, leaned low and shot a blazing arrow into the canvas of the Crockett wagon. Rock fired his right hand pistol and the Indian hit the dirt in a tumbling heap, just as a second arrow knocked off Rock's hat. Reaching up with his left hand, Rock jerked the burning arrow from the canvas. The fire had not yet caught. Then he opened up, firing his pistol, shifting guns, and firing again. The attack broke as suddenly as it had begun.

Tom Crockett was kneeling behind a water barrel, his face gray. A good shot, he was not accustomed to killing. He glanced up at Rock, a sickened expression on his face.

"I never killed nothing human before!" he said weakly.

"You'll get used to it out here," Rock said coldly. His eyes lifted to Sharon.

"You saved our wagon!" she said.

"It might have been anybody's wagon," he said bluntly, and turned away. He counted seven dead Indians on the prairie. There were probably one or two more hidden in the tall grass. He could see several dead ponies. The Indian who had shot the flaming arrow lay not more than a dozen feet away. The bullet had gone through his stomach and broken his spine.

Rock walked around. He had eyes only for the men. Cap looked frightened, but determined. Pagones had fired steadily and with skill. Bannon nodded at the short man.

"You'll do," he said grimly.

Pagones started to speak, stared after him, and scowled a little. He was ashamed of himself when he realized he was pleased at the compliment.

They were good men, Rock decided. Purcell was reloading his rifle, and he looked up as Bannon passed, but said nothing. Rock walked back to the Crockett wagon. Cap was standing there, his rifle in the hollow of his arm.

"Will they come again?" he asked.

Bannon nodded. "Prob'ly several times. This is Buffalo Hide. Those were his warriors."

"But Morton said—" Crockett started to protest.

Bannon looked around, then he pointed at the dead Indian. "You goin' to believe Morton Harper, or that?" he demanded. "That Indian's a Blackfoot. I know by the moccasins."

The next time they came in a circle, going around and around the wagon train. A volley of flaming arrows set two wagon tops afire. Rock stood at the end of the wagon and fired steadily, carefully, making every shot count.

Dawn came with a red, weird light flaming in the east and turning the wagon colors to flame. Guns crashed and the air was filled with wild Indian yells and the acrid smell of gunpowder and burned canvas. Three times more they attacked, and Bannon was everywhere, firing, firing, firing. Crockett went down with a bullet through his thigh. Bjornsen was shot through the head, and a warrior leaped from a horse into Greaves's wagon and the two men fought there until the Indian thrust a knife into Greaves's side. Bannon shot the brave with a snapped pistol shot, almost from the hip.

The last attack broke, and the sun lifted into the sky. As if by magic the Indians were gone. Rock Bannon wiped the sweat from his forehead and stared out over the plain. Buffalo Hide had lost men in this fight. At least twenty of his braves were dead; there would be wailing and the death chant in Blackfoot villages tonight.

Two horses and an ox had been killed. They gathered around, buried the two dead men and butchered the ox. Rock sat on a wagon tongue alone. Cap walked over to him. The man's face was round and uncomfortable.

"Reckon you saved us, Rock," he said. "Don't rightly know how to thank you!"

Bannon got up. He had been cleaning his rifle and reloading it while the men were buried. "Don't try," he said.

Bob Sprague walked over and held out his hand. "Guess we haven't been very friendly," he said, "but you were right about the Indians."

Suddenly, boyishly, Bannon grinned. "Forget it, Bob! You did a good job with that rifle of yours!"

They were the only two who mentioned it. Rock helped lift Crockett into the back of the wagon, then harnessed the oxen. He had already gone, riding flank on the steeldust, when Sharon came to thank him. She looked after him, and her heart felt strangely lost and alone.

It was late that day when they reached the dry country. The settlers did not realize the change until the dust began to rise, for in the distance it had looked much the same, only the grass was darker and there was less of it. Within a mile they were suffused in a cloud of powdery, sifting dust, stifling and irritating in the heat.

This was no desert, but merely long miles of plain where the hills receded, and there was no sub-irrigation to keep the grass green and rich. All the following day the dust cloud hung over the wagon train, and from Mulholland's place in the van the last wagons could not even be distinguished.

Mulholland looked up at Bannon, who was riding beside him. "Harper said there was one bad stretch," he said, almost apologetically.

Bannon did not reply. He alone of all the party knew what lay ahead. He alone knew how brutal the passage would be. Let them find out. . . .

Days later, when Cap asked him to go for game, they all knew. They were still in that desert of dust and dirty brown brush. They had camped in it for five days now. Their water barrels were empty, the wagons so hard to pull in the thick dust that they made only a few miles each day. It was the worst kind of tough going.

When he had killed two antelope in the hills, Rock rode back to join the party. Pagones, hunting on the other side, had killed one. Rock turned toward Sharon's wagon and swung down from the saddle. She looked up at him from over a fire of greasewood.

"Hello," she said. "We haven't seen much of you."

He took off his black, flat-brimmed hat. His dark curly hair was plastered to his brow with sweat.

"There are some here who don't want me talking to you," he said dryly. "Figure I'm a bad influence, I guess."

"I haven't said that!" she protested. She brushed a strand of hair from her eyes. "I like to have you riding close. It—it makes me feel safer."

He looked at her for an instant, then looked away. "How's your dad?"

"Better, I think. But this heat is so awful. How long before we get out of this dust?"

"Tomorrow night, at this rate. This bad stretch is about over."

"Then we're free of that. Morton said there was only one."

He noticed that she had called Harper by his first name. "He was wrong. You'll strike another near Salt Lake that's much worse than this. You'll never get across unless you swing back and take the old trail for Pilot Peak."

"But he said—" Sharon protested.

Rock Bannon looked up at her from where he squatted on his haunches. "I know he did. I heard everything he said, and I'm still wondering what he has to gain by it. Nobody takes this route. Crossing the Salt Desert this way is suicide—with wagons, at least. You've all placed a lot of faith in a stranger!"

"He was right, Rock. Those first six days were heaven, and from now on it should be good."

"From now on it will be good until you hit the desert," he admitted; "unless you stop."

"Unless we stop?" Sharon dished up a plate and handed it to him, then poured the coffee. "Why?"

"Tomorrow we get into Hardy Bishop's country." Rock Bannon's face was somber.

"You always refer to him as if he were an outlaw, or something awful!"

"No," he said. "Bishop isn't that. If you are his friend, or a guest, he's one of the finest men alive. If you are an enemy or try to take something that's his, he is absolutely ruthless."

When she returned from feeding her father, she sat down beside him on the wagon tongue. The sun was down, and the dust settled. Near a fire on the far side of the circle Dud Kitchen was singing softly over his mandolin.

The air was cool now, and the soft music mingled in the air with the scent of woodsmoke and the low champing of the horses or the mumbling of the oxen. In the distance they could see the hills, purple with last shadows before darkness, and shadowed with a promise of coolness after the long days of heat and dust and bitterness.

He stared away at the hills, remembering so much, worried, uncertain, wondering again about Morton Harper. What did the man have in mind? Who was he? Purcell had said he had lent him money. It was not like a man to lend money and not follow it up to get back what was his. Behind all of this was a reason, and in the back of his mind Rock was afraid he knew that reason.

Sharon spoke suddenly. "What are you thinking of, Rock? You're always so silent. You seem so bitter sometimes, and I can never understand what you have on your mind."

"It isn't anything." He had no desire to mention Harper again. "I was just thinking about this country."

"You like it, don't you?"

"Like it?" He looked up suddenly, and his eyes changed. He smiled suddenly and with warmth. "Like it? I love it! This is a man's country! And that ahead? Wait until you see Bishop's Valley! Miles upon miles of tumbling streams, and waving green grass dotted with cattle!

"You should see Bishop's Valley! You go down through a deep gorge along a roaring mountain stream, and you can look up at cliffs that rise for three thousand feet, and then suddenly the gorge widens and you look down a long valley that's six or seven miles wide and all of fifty miles long.

"On each side high mountain ridges shut it in, and here and there deep gorges and ravines cut back into those ridges and there are green meadows and tumbling waterfalls. And all the hills around are timbered to their crests. It's a beautiful country!"

Sharon stared at him, enchanted. Rock had never talked like this before, and as she listened to him tell of the hills and the wild game, of deer, elk, bear and mountain goats, of the catbirds calling in the willows and the hillsides white with groves of silver-columned birch, she suddenly forgot where she was, or who was talking.

"You seem to love it so much!" she said. "Why did you ever leave?"

"It belongs to one man—to Hardy Bishop," Rock said. "He's carving a little empire here. He went there long before any other white man dreamed of anything but going on to California, before they thought of anything but getting rich from gold mines. They came through the country like a pack of vultures, taking everything, building nothing. They want only to get rich and get out.

"He was different. Once, when only a boy, he went into that valley on a trapping venture, and he was never content until he came back. He drove a herd of cattle west when there were no cattle in this country, and he got them into that valley and turned them loose. He fought Indians and outlaws, he built a dam, built a home, built irrigation ditches where he wanted them and planted trees.

"He made the valley, and you can't blame him if he wants to keep it his way now."

Long after Sharon lay in her blankets she thought of that, and of Rock Bannon. How tall he was! And how strange! He had risen suddenly, and with scarcely a word had walked into the night, and then she heard him mount his horse and ride away. Yet even as she heard the dwindling hoofbeats, she heard something else. The sound of other horses, drawing near. Still wondering who they could be, she fell asleep. . . .

Scarcely were they moving in the morning before a black mare wheeled alongside her wagon. Flushing suddenly, she saw Morton Harper, hat in hand, bowing to her.

"Good morning!" he said. "I hoped to catch up with you before this, but by tomorrow you'll be in green country again!"

"Yes, I know."

He looked at her quickly. "You know? Who told you?"

"Rock Bannon."

His face sharpened, and she could sense the irritation in the man. "Oh? Then he's still with you? I was hoping he had left you alone. I'm afraid he's not a good man."

"Why do you say that? He's been very helpful."

Harper shrugged. "I'd rather not say. You know of that killing in Laramie, and if that were the only one, it would not matter. There are others. He has killed five or six men. He's a troublemaker wherever he goes. I'm glad Purcell and your men understand that, for it will save a lot of trouble."

He smiled at her. "You look so lovely this morning that it's unbelievable that you have come so far across the prairie. It is a pity you have so far to go. I've been thinking some of settling in this country here." He waved ahead. "It is such a beautiful land, and there is nothing in California so desirable."

Rock Bannon had heard the horses the night before, and he reined in long enough to see them come up to the fire. Harper he recognized at once. There were two men with him, one a lean, sharp-faced man with a long nose. The other man was short, chuckleheaded and blunt featured. Bannon's lips tightened when he recognized Pete Zapata. The half-breed killer was notorious, a gunfighter and desperado of the worst stripe, but none of the wagon train would know that.

All that day he stayed away from the train, riding on ahead. He drank at the spring, killed an antelope and a couple of teal, then rode back under a clump of poplars and waited for the wagon train to come up. They were already on Hardy Bishop's V Bar. Only a short distance behind the poplars, the long canyon known as Poplar Canyon ran down into Bishop's Valley.

He got up when he saw the first of the long caravan of wagons. Better than the others, he knew what this would mean, and knew on how bad a trail they had started. He was standing there, close to the stallion, when the wagons moved in.

The fresh water and green grass made everyone happy. Brown-legged children rushed downstream from where the drinking water was obtained, and there was laughter and merrymaking in the camp. Fires sprang up, and in a short time the camp was made and meals were being cooked.

Watchfully, Rock saw Morton Harper seated on a

saddle at Cap Mulholland's fire. With them were the sharp-featured stranger, Satterfield, and Lamport and Pagones. They were deep in a conference. In a few minutes Tom Crockett walked over to join them.

Dud Kitchen was tuning his mandolin when he saw Bannon sitting under the willows.

"All alone?" Kitchen said with a grin, and dropped on the grass beside Bannon. "Saw how you handled those guns in that Indian fight. Never saw the like. Made more tune with 'em than me with a mandolin!"

Rock chuckled. "But not so nice to hear." He nodded at the group of men around the fire. "Wonder what's up?"

Dud shrugged. "Harper's got some plan he's talkin' about. Sayin' they are foolish to go on when there's good country right here."

Rock Bannon sprang to his feet, his eyes afire with apprehension. "So that's it?" he said. "I might have known it!"

Kitchen was startled. "What's the matter? I think it would be a good idea, myself. This is beautiful country. I don't know that I've ever seen better. Harper says that down this draw behind us there's a long, beautiful valley, all open for settlement."

But Rock Bannon was no longer listening. Stepping across the branch of the creek, he started for the fire. Morton Harper was talking when Rock walked up.

"Why not?" Harper was saying. "You all want homes. Can you find a more beautiful country than this? That dry plain is behind you. Ahead lies the Salt Lake Desert, but in here—this is a little bit of paradise. Beyond this range of hills—you can reach it through Poplar Canyon— is the most beautiful valley you ever saw. It's just crying for people to come in and settle down! There's game in the hills, the best grazing land in the world, all for the taking!"

"What about Hardy Bishop?" Bannon demanded. Harper looked up, angered. "You again? Every time these people try to do anything, you interfere! Is it your business where they stop? Is it your business if they remain here or go on to California? Are you trying to dictate to them?"

Pike Purcell was on his feet, and Rock could see all the old dislike in the big Missourian's face. The other men looked at him with disapproval, too. Yet he went on recklessly, heedlessly.

"Hardy Bishop settled that valley, and he's running two thousand head of cattle in there. You try to settle in that valley and you're asking for trouble. He won't stand for it."

"An' we won't stand for you buttin' in!" Purcell said suddenly. He dropped a hand to the big dragoon pistol in his holster. "I've had enough of you interferin' in our affairs. I'm tellin' you now, you shut up an' get out."

"Wait a minute!" Bob Sprague stepped closer. "This man warned us about that Indian attack or we'd all be dead, includin' you, Pike Purcell. He did more fightin' in that attack than any one of us, or any two of us, for that matter. His advice has been good, and I think we should listen to him!"

Dud Kitchen nodded. "Speak up, Rock. I'll listen!"

"There's little to be said," Bannon told them quietly. "Only the land this man is suggesting you settle on was settled on over ten years ago by a man who fought Indians to get it. He fought Indians and outlaws to keep it. He won't see it taken from him now in his old age. I know Hardy Bishop. I know him well enough to be sure that if you move into that valley many of the women in this wagon train will be widows before the year is out.

"What I don't know is Morton Harper's reason for urging you into this. I don't know why he urged you to take this trail, but I think he has a reason, and I think that reason lies in Bishop's Valley. You're coming west to win homes. You have no right to do it by taking what another man fought to win and to keep. There is plenty for all further west."

"That makes sense to me," Sprague said quietly. "I for one am moving west!"

"Well, I'm not!" Purcell said stubbornly. "I like this country, and me and the wife have seen enough dust and sun and Indians! We aim to stay!"

"That valley is fifty miles long, gentlemen," Harper said. "I think there's room enough for us all in Bishop's Valley."

"That seems right to me!" Cap said. He looked around at Tom Crockett, limping near the fire. "How about you, Tom?"

"I'm staying," Crockett said. "I like it here."

Satterfield nodded. "Reckon I'll find me a place to set up a blacksmith shop," he said. "But there's a sight of things we all need. There ain't no stores, no place to get some things we figured to get in California."

"That will be where I come in." The man with the sharp features smiled pleasantly. "I'm John Kies, and I have six wagonloads of goods coming over the trail to open a store in our new town!"

Silently, Rock Bannon turned away. There was no further use in talking. He caught Sharon's eye, but she looked away, her gaze drawn to Mort Harper where he sat now, talking easily, smoothly, planning the new homes, the new town.

Bannon walked back to his blankets and turned in, listening to the whispering of the poplar leaves and the soft murmur of the water in the branch. It was a long time before he fell asleep, long after the last talking had died away in the wagon train, and when the fires had burned low.

III

THEN DAYLIGHT came, Rock Bannon bathed, and saddled the stallion. Then carefully, he checked his guns. At a sound, he glanced up to see Sharon Crockett dipping water from the stream.

"Good morning," he said. "Did you finally decide to stay?"

"Yes." She stepped toward him. "Rock, why are you always against everything we do? Why don't you stay, too? I'm sure Morton would be glad to have you. He's planned all this so well, and he says we'll need good men. Why don't you join us?"

"No, not this time. I stayed with the wagon train because I knew what you were going into. I wanted to help you—and I mean you. In what is to come, no one can help you. Besides, my heart wouldn't be in it."

"You're afraid of this crabby old man?" she asked scornfully. "Morton says as soon as Bishop sees that we intend to stay, he won't oppose us at all! He's just difficult because he's old, and he has more land than he needs. Are you afraid of him?"

Rock smiled. "You sure set a lot of store by this Harper fellow, don't you? Did he tell you that Bishop's riders were all crabby old men, too? Did Harper tell you why he carries Pete Zapata along with him?"

"Who is he?" Sharon looked up, her eyes curious, yet resentful.

"You've called me a killer," Bannon replied. "I have killed men. I may kill more, although I hope not. But Pete Zapata, that flat-faced half-breed who rides with Harper, is a murderer. He's a killer of the most vicious type, and the kind of man no decent man would have near him!"

Her eyes flared. "You don't think Morton Harper is

decent? How dare you say such a thing behind his back?"

"I'll face him with it," Bannon said dryly. "I expect I'll face him with it more than once. But before you get in too deep, ask yourself again what he's getting out of all this. He goes in for talk of brotherly love, but he carries a gunman at his elbow!"

He turned and swung into the saddle as she picked up her bucket. He reined in the horse at a call. It was Bob Sprague.

"Hey, Rock! Want to come on west with us?"

He halted. "You're going on?"

"Uh-huh. Six wagons are going. We decided we liked the sound of what you said. We're pullin' on for Californy, and we'd sure like to have you with us!"

Bannon hesitated. Sharon was walking away, her head held proudly. Did she seem to hesitate for his reply? He shrugged.

"No," he said. "I've got other plans."

Sharon Crockett, making frying-pan bread over the fire beside her wagon, stood up to watch Bob Sprague lead off the six wagons, the owners of which had decided not to stay. All farewells had been said the night before, yet now that time for the leavetaking had come, she watched uneasily.

For years she had known Bob Sprague, ever since she was a tiny girl. He had been her father's friend, a steady, reliable man, and now he was going. With him went five other families, and among them some of the steadiest, soberest men in the lot.

Were they wrong to take Morton Harper's advice? Her father, limping with the aid of a cane cut from the willows, walked back and stood beside her, his face somber. He was a tall man, almost as tall as Harper or Bannon, his hair silvery around the temples, his face gray with a slight stubble of beard. He was a fearless, independent man, given to going his own way, and thinking his own thoughts.

Pagones walked over to them. "Did Bannon go along? I ain't seen him."

"I don't think he went," Crockett replied. "Sprague wanted him to go."

"No, he didn't go," said Satterfield, who had walked up to join them. Satterfield had been a frontier lawyer back in Illinois. "I saw him riding off down the canyon, maybe an hour ago."

"You think there will be trouble?" Pagones asked.

Satterfield shrugged. "Probably not. I know how some of these old frontiersmen are. They hate to see civilization catch up with them, but given time, they come around. Where's Harper?"

"He went off somewhere with that dark-lookin' feller who trails with him," Pagones said. "Say, I'm glad Dud Kitchen didn't go. I'd sure miss that music he makes. He was goin', then at the last minute changed his mind. He's goin' down with Harper and Cap to survey that town site."

"Seem good to have a town again," Crockett said. "Where's it to be?"

"Down where Poplar Canyon runs into Bishop's Valley. Wide, beautiful spot, they say, with plenty of water and grass. John Kies is puttin' in a store, I'm going to open an office, and Collins is already figurin' on a blacksmith shop."

"Father, did you ever hear of a man named Zapata?" Sharon asked thoughtfully. "Pete Zapata?"

Crockett looked at her curiously. "Why, no. Not that I recall. Why?"

"I was just wondering."

The next morning they hitched up the oxen and moved their ten wagons down Poplar Canyon to the townsite. The high, rocky walls of the canyon widened slowly, and the oxen walked on, knee deep in rich, green grass. Along the stream were willow and poplar, and higher along the canyon sides Sharon saw alder, birch and mountain mahogany with here and there a fine stand of lodgepole pine.

Tom Crockett was driving, so she ranged alongside, riding her sorrel mare.

As they rounded the last bend in the canyon, it spread wide before them and she saw Morton Harper sitting his black mare some distance off. Putting the sorrel to a gallop, she rode down swiftly, hair blowing in the wind. Dud Kitchen was there with Zapata and Cap. They were driving stakes and lining up a street.

Before them the valley dropped into the great open space of Bishop's Valley, and she rode on. Suddenly, rounding a knoll, she stopped and caught her breath.

The long, magnificent sweep of the valley lay before her, green and splendid in the early-morning sun. Here and there over the grassland cattle grazed, belly deep in the tall grass. It was overpowering, it was breathtaking. It was something beyond the grasp of the imagination. High on either side lifted the soaring walls of the canyon, mounting into high ridges, snow-capped peaks, and majestic walls of gray rock.

This was the cattle empire of Hardy Bishop. This was the place Rock Bannon spoke of with such amazing eloquence.

She turned in her saddle at the sound of a horse's hoofs. Mort Harper rode up beside her, his face glowing.

"Look!" he cried. "Magnificent, isn't it? The most beautiful view in the world. Surely that's an empire worth taking!"

Sharon's head turned quickly, sharply. At something in Harper's eyes she caught her breath, and when she looked again at the valley, she was uneasy.

"What—what did you say?" she asked. "An empire worth taking?"

He glanced at her quickly, then laughed. "Don't pay any mind. I was thinking of Bishop, the man who claims all this. He took it. Took it from the Indians by main force." Then he added, "He's an old brute. He'd stop at nothing!"

"Do you think he'll make trouble for us?" she inquired anxiously.

He shrugged. "Probably not. He might, but if he does, we can handle that part of it. Let's go back, shall we?"

She was silent during the return ride, and she kept turning over in her mind her memory of Bannon's question, "What's he going to get out of this?" Somehow, half hypnotized by Harper's eloquence, she had not really thought of that. That she thought of it now gave her a twinge of doubt. It seemed somehow disloyal.

For three days life in the new town went on briskly. They named the town Poplar, and Kies's store was the first building up, and the shelves were heavy with goods and needed things. Kies was smiling and affable. "Don't worry about payment!" he assured them. "We're all in this together! Just get what you need and I'll put it on the books, then when you get money from furs or crops you can pay me!"

It was easy. It was almost too easy. Tom Crockett built a house in a bend of the creek among the trees, and he bought dress goods for Sharon, trousers for himself, bacon and flour. Then he bought some new tools.

Those first three days were hard, unrelenting labor, yet joyful labor, too. They were building homes, and there is always something warming and pleasant in that. At the end of those first three days, Kies's store was up, Collins's blacksmith shop, Satterfield's office, and Hardy's Saloon and Theater. All of them pitched in, and all of them worked.

Then one day, as Sharon was leaving Kies's store, she looked up to see three strange horsemen coming down the street. They were walking their horses, and they were looking around in ill-concealed amazement.

Mulholland had come out behind her, and at the sight of him, one of the horsemen, a big, stern-looking man with a drooping red mustache, reined his horse around.

"You!" he said. "What do you all think you're doin' here?"

"Buildin' us a town," Cap said aggressively. "Any objections?"

Red laughed sardonically. "Well, sir," he said, "I reckon I haven't, but I'm afraid the boss is sure goin' to raise hob!"

"Who's the boss?" Cap asked. "And what difference does it make? This is all free land, isn't it?"

"The boss is Hardy Bishop," Red drawled, glancing around. He looked approvingly at Sharon, and there seemed a glint of humor in his eyes. "And you say this is free land. It is, and it ain't. You see, out here a man takes what he can hold. Hardy come in here when all you folks was livin' fat and comfortable back in the States. He settled here, and he worked hard. He trapped and hunted and washed him some color, and then he went back to the States and bought cattle. Drivin' them cattle out here ten years ago was sure a chore, folks, but he done it. Now they've bred into some of the biggest herds in the country. I don't think Hardy's goin' to like you folks movin' in here like this."

"Is he so selfish?" Sharon demanded. "Why, there's land here enough for thousands of people!"

Red looked at her. "That's how you see it, ma'am. I reckon to your way of thinkin', back East, that might be true. Here, it ain't true. A man's needs run accordin' to the country he's in and the job he has to do. Hardy Bishop is runnin' cows. He expects to supply beef for thousands of people. To do that he needs a lot of land. You see, ma'am, if thousands of people can't raise their own beef, somebody's got to have land enough to raise beef for them. And Hardy, he come by it honest."

"By murdering Indians, I suppose!"

Red looked at her thoughtfully. "Ma'am, somebody's been tellin' you wrong. Plumb wrong. Hardy never murdered no Indians."

"What's going on here?" Morton Harper stepped into the street. To his right was Pete Zapata, to his left Pike Purcell. Lamport lounged in the door of the store.

"Why, nothin', mister," Red said thoughtfully. His gaze had sharpened, and Sharon saw his eyes go from Harper to Zapata. "We was just talkin' about land and the ownership of it. We're ridin' for Bishop, and—"

"And you can ride right out of here!" Harper snapped. "Now!"

Sharon was closer to the Bishop riders, and she heard the second man say softly: "Watch it, Red! That's Zapata!"

Red seemed to stiffen in his saddle and his hand, which had started to slip off the pommel of the saddle, with no aggressive intention, froze in position. Without a word, they turned their horses and rode away.

"That's the beginning," Harper stated positively. "I'm afraid they mean to drive us from our homes!"

"They didn't sound much like trouble," Cap ventured, hesitantly. "Talked mighty nice!"

"Don't be fooled by them!" Harper warned. "Bishop is an outlaw, or the next thing to it. . . ."

Tom Crockett was a man who loved the land. No sooner had he put a plow into the deep, rich soil of the canyon bottom than he felt he had indeed come home. The soil, deep and black, heavy with richness, a land that had never known a plow. Working early and late, he had in the next day managed to plow several acres. The seed he bought from Kies, who seemed to have everything they needed.

There were several hours a day he gave to working on the buildings the others were throwing up, but logs were handy, and all but Zapata and Kies worked on the felling and notching of them. Kies stayed in his store, and Zapata lounged close by.

Morton Harper helped with the work, but Sharon noticed that he was never without a gun, and his rifle was always close by. At night in his saloon he played cards with Purcell and Lamport and anyone else who came around. Yet several times a day he managed to stop by, if only for a minute, to talk to her.

He stopped one day when she was planting a vine near the door. He watched her for a few minutes, and then he stepped closer.

"Sharon," he said gently. "You shouldn't be doing this sort of thing. You're too beautiful. Why don't you let me take care of you?"

She looked at him, suddenly serious. "Is this a proposal?"

His eyes flashed, then he smiled. "What else? I suppose I'm pretty clumsy at it."

"No," she returned thoughtfully, "you're not clumsy at it, but let's wait. Let's not talk about it until everyone has a home and is settled in a place of their own."

"All right," he agreed reluctantly. "But that won't be very long, you know."

It was not until they were eating supper that night that her thoughts suddenly offered her a question. What about Morton's home? He had not even started to build. He was sleeping in a room behind the saloon, such in name only as yet, for there was little liquor to be had.

The thought had not occurred to her before, but it puzzled and disturbed her. Tom Crockett was full of plans, talking of crops and the rich soil.

The next day Morton Harper was gone. Where he had gone Sharon did not know, but suddenly, in the middle of the morning she realized he was not among them, and the black mare was gone, too. Shortly after noon she saw him riding into town, and behind him came six wagons, loaded with boxes and barrels. They drew up before the store and the saloon.

He saw her watching and loped the mare over to her door.

"See?" he said, waving a hand. "The supplies! Everything we need for the coming year, but if we need more, I can send a rider back to the fort."

"Then you had them coming from the fort?" she asked. "You were far-sighted."

He laughed, glancing at her quickly. "Well, I thought these things would sell in the mining camps out in California, but this is much, much better."

In spite of herself, Sharon was disturbed. All day as she went about her work the thought kept recurring that those supplies offered a clue to something, yet she could find nothing on which to fasten her suspicions. Why should their arrival disturb her so much. Was it unusual that a man should start several wagon loads of supplies to California?

Pagones stopped by the spring to get a drink. He smiled at her, pushing back his hat from a sweating brow.

"Lots of work, ma'am. Your pa's sure getting in his plowing in a hurry. He'll have his seed in before the rest of us have started."

"Pag, how do the supplies reach the gold fields in California?" Sharon said suddenly.

He looked up over his second dipper of water. "Why, by sea, of course! Much cheaper that way. Why do you ask? Something botherin' you?"

"Not exactly. Only ever since those wagons came in this morning, I've been wondering about them. Morton said he had started them for California, but thought they would sell better here. Why would he send them to California to sell when they can get supplies easier by sea?"

"Might mean a little ready money," Pagones suggested. He hung the dipper on a shrub. "Now that you mention it, it does seem kind of strange."

The expected trouble from Hardy Bishop did not materialize as soon as she expected. No other riders came near, although several times she noticed men, far out in the valley. All Morton Harper's promises seemed to be coming true. He had said Bishop would not bother them.

Yet all was not going too smoothly. The last wagons had brought a load of liquor, and several of the men hung around the saloon most of the time. Purcell was there every evening, although by day he worked on his place. Pete Zapata was always there when not off on one of his lonely rides, and the teamsters who had brought the wagons to Kies's store had remained, loitering about, doing nothing at all, but always armed. One of them had become the bartender.

During all this time her work had kept Sharon close to the house, and there had been no time for riding. Time and again she found herself going to the door and looking down toward the cluster of buildings that was fast becoming a thriving little village. And just as often she looked back up the trail they had followed when first coming into Poplar Canyon.

Not even to herself would she admit what she was looking for. She refused to admit that she longed to see the steel-dust stallion and its somber, lonely rider. She had overheard him say he would not leave, yet where was he?

The sound of horse's hoofs in the trail outside brought her to the cabin door. It was Mary Pagones, daughter of George Pagones, who had long since proved himself one of the most stable men in the wagon train.

"Come on, Sharon—let's ride! I'm beginning to feel cramped with staying down here all the time."

Sharon needed no urging, and in a few minutes they were riding out of the settlement toward the upper reaches of the canyon.

"Have you seen that Pete Zapata staring at the women the way he does?" Mary asked. "He fairly gives me the creeps!"

"Somebody said he was a gunman," Sharon ventured.

"I wouldn't doubt it!" Mary was an attractive girl, always gay and full of laughter. The freckles over her nose were an added attraction rather than otherwise. "Dud doesn't like him at all. Says he can't see why Harper keeps him around."

As they rode out of Poplar Canyon, an idea suddenly occurred to Sharon, and without voicing it she turned her mare toward their old encampment, but as they burst through the last line of trees, disappointment flooded over her. There was no sign of Rock Bannon.

They had gone almost a mile further, when suddenly Mary reined in sharply.

"Why, look at that!" She pointed. "Wagon tracks coming out of that canyon! Who in the world would ever take a wagon in there?"

Sharon looked at them, then at the canyon. It was narrow-mouthed, the only entrance into a wild, rugged region of crags and ravines, heavily forested and forbidding. Riding closer, she looked down. The wagon tracks were coming from the canyon, not going into it. She studied the mountains thoughtfully, then wheeling her horse, with Mary following, she rode out on their own trail. All the tracks she had observed were old.

She looked at Mary, and Mary returned the glance, a puzzled frown gathering around her eyes. "What's the matter?" Mary asked. "Is something wrong?"

"I don't know," Sharon said. "There are no tracks here since we came over the trail, but there are tracks coming out of that canyon!"

Mary's eyes widened. "You mean those wagons of

Harper's? Then they must have come over a different trail."

That wasn't what Sharon was thinking, but she just shook her head. "Don't say anything about it," she said. They rode on. That wall of mountain would not offer a trail through, and if it did, where would it go? If it joined the Overland Trail to the north, it would still be almost twice as far as by the trail they had come, and through one of the most rugged sections she had ever seen. Suddenly, she knew. Those wagons had been here before. They had been back there, in some remote canyon, waiting.

Waiting for what? For a town to begin? But that was absurd. No one had known the town would begin until a few hours before. No one, unless it had been Morton Harper.

On, through hills of immeasurable beauty, the two girls rode. Great, rocky escarpments that towered to the skies, and mighty crags, breasting their saw-toothed edges against the wind. Long, steep hillsides clad with alder and birch, or rising to great, dark, feathered crests of lodgepole pine mingled here and there with an occasional fir.

Along the lower hillsides and along the mountain draws were quaking aspen, mountain mahogany and hawthorn. They had come to the edge of a grove of poplar when they saw the horseman. They both saw him at once, and something in his surreptitious manner brought them to a halt. They both recognized him at the same instant.

"Sharon," Mary said, "it's that Zapata!"

"S-sh! He'll hear us!" Sharon held her breath. Suddenly, she was frightened at the idea of being found out here, even with Mary along, by the half-breed. But Zapata seemed to have no eyes for them, or even for their direction. He was riding by very slowly, not over fifty yards away, carrying his rifle in his hands, and watching something in the valley below which was beyond their vision.

Yet even as they watched he slid suddenly from the

saddle and crouched upon some rocks on the rim. Then he lifted his rifle and fired!

"What's he shooting at?" Mary asked in a whisper.

"I don't know. A deer probably. Let's go home."

Turning their horses they rode back through the trees and hit the trail back to the settlement.

IV

ALL THE NEXT DAY Sharon thought about that wagon trail out of the mountains. Several times she started to speak to her father, but he was preoccupied, lost in plans for his new home, and thinking of nothing but it. Later in the day she saw Dud Kitchen riding over. He reined in and slid from the saddle.

"Howdy, Sharon! Sure glad to see you! We been talkin' home, Mary and I, about gettin' up a sort of party. Seems like Satterfield plays a fiddle, and we thought we might have a dance, sort of. Liven things up a mite."

"That's a good idea, Dud," Sharon agreed. She looked up at him suddenly. "Dud, did Mary tell you anything about that wagon trail we saw?"

His blue eyes sharpened and he ran his fingers back through his corn-colored hair. "Yeah," he said, "she did."

"Dud, it looks to me as if those wagons were out here before we were, just waiting. It begins to look as if somebody planned to have us stop here."

"You mean Mort? But what would he do that for? What could he gain? And even if he did, you got to admit it's a good place."

"Yes, it is, but just the same I don't like it."

Her father was walking toward them with George Pagones and Cap Mulholland.

"What's this you young folks figurin' to do?" Cap said, grinning. "Hear we're havin' us a party?"

Her answer was drowned by a sudden rattle of horses' hoofs and she saw three men swing down the canyon trail. When the saw the group before the house, they reined in. One of the man was Red, the man who had called on them the first day. Another was—her breath caught—Rock Bannon!

"Howdy!" Red said. He looked down at the men, then

recognized Cap. "Seen anything of a young fellow, 'bout twenty, or so, ridin' a bay pony?"

"Why no," Cap said. "Can't say as I have. What's the trouble?"

"He's Wes Freeman, who rides for us. He was huntin' strays over this way yesterday and he never came back. We figured maybe he was hurt somehow."

"No, we haven't seen him," Crockett said.

Dud Kitchen was grinning at Rock. "Shucks, man! We figured you had left the country. What you doin'?"

Bannon grinned. "I'm ridin' for Hardy Bishop," he said. "Went over there right after I left you folks."

"What made you think your man might have come over here?" Pagones asked. "Was he ridin' this way?"

"As a matter of fact," Red said, "he was ridin' back northeast of here. Pretty rough country, except for one canyon that's got some good grass in it."

The third man was short, thick-set and tough. "Hurry up, Red!" he said. "Why beat around the brush. Tell 'em!"

"All right," Red said. "I'll do just that, Bat!" He looked down at the little group before the house. "Fact the matter is, Wes's horse come in about sundown yesterday, come in with blood on the saddle. We back-trailed the horse and we found Wes. We found him in the open valley we spoke of. He was dead. He'd been shot through the back and knocked off his horse. Then whoever shot him had followed him up and killed him with a hunting knife."

Zapata! Sharon's eyes widened, and she looked around to see Dud staring at her, gray-faced. She had seen Zapata shoot!

In stunned silence the men stared up at the three riders. Rock broke the silence.

"You can see what this means?" he said sternly. "Wes was a mighty nice boy. I hadn't know him as long as these men, but he seemed to be a right fine kid. Now he's been murdered—drygulched. That's going to mean trouble."

"But why come to us?" Cap protested. "You don't believe we—"

"We don't believe!" Bat broke in harshly. "We know! We trailed three riders down out of those hills! Three from here! Wes was my ridin' partner. He was a durned good boy. I'm goin' to see the man who done that."

"Turn around."

The voice was cold and deadly. As one person, they turned. Pete Zapata, his guns low-slung on his hips, was staring at the three riders. Flanking him were two men with shotguns, both of them from the teamsters' crowd. The other two were Lamport and Purcell, of the wagon train. Behind them, and a little to one side, was Morton Harper. He was wearing two guns.

"Get out of here!" Harper snapped harshly. "Don't come around here again, aimin' to make trouble. That's all you came for, and you know it! You've been looking for an excuse to start something so you could get us out of here, take our homes away from us. Now turn your horses and get out!"

His eyes riveted on Rock Bannon. "As for you, Bannon," he said sharply, "you're a traitor! You rode with us, and now you've gone over to them. I think you're the cause of all this trouble. If a man of yours is dead, I think it would be a good idea if these friends of yours back-trailed you. Now get moving, all of you!"

"This is a bad mistake, Harper," Rock said evenly. "I'm speaking of it before all these people." He nodded at the group in front of the house. "Bishop was inclined to let 'em stay, despite the fact that he was afraid they'd bring more after them. He listened to me, and didn't run you off. Now you're asking for it."

"He listened to you!" Harper's voice was alive with contempt. "You? A trail-runner?"

Red looked quickly at Rock and started to speak.

Bannon silenced him with a gesture. "We'll ride, Harper, but we want the man—or men—who killed Wes. And we want him delivered to us by sundown tomorrow! If not, we'll come and get him."

Turning abruptly, they started away. Wheeling Zapata grabbed a shotgun from one of the teamsters. "I'll fix him, the bluffer!"

"Hold it!" Pagones had a six-shooter and was staring across it at Zapata. "We don't shoot men in the back."

For an instant, they glared at each other. Then Harper interposed. "Put it down, Pete. Let them go." He looked around. "There'll be a meeting at the saloon tonight. All of you be there."

When they had all gone, Tom Crokett shook his head sadly. "More trouble, and all because of that Bannon. I almost wish we'd let him die on the trail."

"It wasn't Bannon, Father," Sharon said. "Those men were right, I think. Mary and I saw Zapata yesterday. Two of the horses they trailed back here were ours. The other one was his. We weren't fifty yards away from him when he fired that shot. We didn't see what he shot at, but it must have been that man."

Crokett's face was gray. "Are you sure, Sharon? Are you positive?"

"Yes, I am."

"Then we must give him up," he said slowly. "If he killed, he should suffer for it. Especially if he killed that way." He got up and reached for his hat. "I must go and tell Morton. He'll want to know."

She put a hand on his arm. "Father, don't. Don't say anything to him until you've told the others. Pagones, I mean, and Cap. I'm afraid."

"Afraid of what? Morton Harper is a fine man. When he knows what happened, he'll want something done himself."

Putting on his hat, he started across the road for the cluster of buildings. Only for an instant did Sharon hesitate; then she swung around and ran to her horse, standing saddled and bridled, as she had planned to ride over to Mary's. Dud Kitchen would be there, and Pagones.

They were sitting at the table when she burst into the room.

"Please come with me!" she said, when she had explained. "I'm afraid!"

Without a word, they got up and buckled on their guns. It was only a few hundred yards to the saloon, and they arrived just a few minutes after Tom Crockett walked up to Harper.

"Morton, my daughter and Mary Pagones saw Zapata fire that shot yesterday," Crokett was saying. "I think we should surrender him to Bishop. We don't want to have a part in any killings."

Harper's face hardened and he started to speak. Zapata, overhearing his name, stepped to the door, his hand on a gun. Then Harper's face softened a little, and he shrugged.

"I'm afraid they were mistaken," he said carelessly. "You're being needlessly excited. Probably Pete was up that way, for he rides around a good deal, the same as the girls do. But shoot a man in the back? He wouldn't do it."

"Oh, but he did," Dud Kitchen interrupted. "What the girls say is true."

"You call me a liar?" Harper turned on him, his face suddenly flushed with anger.

"No," Kitchen replied stiffly, his face paling. "I ain't callin' a man a liar, especially a man who come over the trail with me. But I know what I seen with my own eyes.

"Mary told me about that, and I'll admit I figured there was something wrong with what she said, so I went up and back-trailed 'em. I didn't have any idea about a killin' then, but I trailed the girls, and then I trailed Pete.

"Pete Zapata stalked that cowhand two miles before he

got the shot he wanted. I went over every inch of his trail. He was fixin' to kill him. Then I trailed him down to the body. I seen where he wiped his knife on the grass, and I seen some of them brown sort of cigarettes he smokes. Pete Zapata killed that man, sure as I'm alive!"

Zapata had walked, cat-footed, to the edge of the wide plank porch in front of the saloon. He stood there now, staring at Dud.

"Trailed me, huh" His hand swept down in a streaking movement before Dud could as much as move. His gun bellowed, and Dud Kitchen turned halfway around and dropped into the dust.

"Why, Mort!" Crockett's face was gray. "What does this mean? I—"

"You'd better all go back to your homes," Harper said sternly. "If Pete Zapata shot that man, and I don't admit for a minute that he did, he had a reason for it. As for this shooting here, Kitchen was wearing a gun, and he accused Zapata of murder."

Pagones' face was hard as stone. Two of the teamsters stood on the porch with shotguns. To have lifted a hand would have been to die.

"That settles it," Pagones said. "You can have your town! I'm leaving!"

"I reckon that goes for me, too," Crockett said sadly.

"I'm afraid you can't go," Harper said smoothly. There was a glint of triumph in his eyes. "My friend, John Kies, has lent you all money and supplies. Unless you can repay him what you owe, you'll have to stay until you have made a crop. California is a long ways off, and he couldn't be sure of collecting there.

"Besides," he added, "Indians have rustled some of our stock. I have been meaning to tell you. Most of your oxen are gone." He shrugged. "But why worry? Stay here. This land is good, and these little difficulties will iron themselves out. There are always troubles when a new community begins. In a few years all this will be over and there will be children born here, a church built, and many homes."

Dud Kitchen was not dead. In the Pagones' house, Mary sat beside his bed. Scatterfield had removed the bullet, and now he sat at the kitchen table, drinking coffee.

"He's got a chance," Scatterfield said. "A good chance. I'm no doctor, just picked up a mite when I was in that Mexican War, but I think he'll come through."

Pagones, his heavy head thrust forward on his thick neck, stared into the fire, sombre, brooding. He turned and looked at Scatterfield and Crockett.

"Well," he said, "it looks bad. Looks like we're in a fight whether we want it or not. Hardy Bishop hasn't bothered us none, even after all of Mort Harper's preaching about him. Now that breed has killed one of his men."

"That Red," Scatterfield muttered, half to himself. "He don't look like no man to have trouble with. Nor Bat, either!"

"Where does Rock stand?" Pagones demanded. "That's what I'm wonderin'."

"Said he was ridin' for Bishop," Scatterfield replied. "That's plain enough."

"If we'd listened to him, this wouldn't have happened," Mary said.

There was no reply to that. The three men stood quiet, listening to Dud Kitchen's heavy breathing. The rap at the door startled them, and they looked up to see Rock Bannon standing there.

Sharon drew in her breath, and she watched him wide-eyed as he stepped into the room and closed the door after him. Hat in hand, his eyes strayed from them to the wounded man lying in the bed.

How tall he was! And his shoulders had seemed to fill the door when he entered. He wore buckskin trousers tucked into hand-tooled star boots, and checked shirt with a buckskin jacket, Mexican fashion, over it. On his hips were two dragoon Colts in tied-down holsters.

"He hurt bad?" he asked softly.

"Yes, but Jim Scatterfield says he's got a chance," Mary said.

Rock Bannon turned to look at them. "Well," he said, "you saw me ride in here today. You know I'm riding for Bishop. From what's happened, I reckon you know that war's been declared. You've got to make up your mind whose side you're on. I talked Hardy Bishop into lettin' you stay on, against his better judgment. He was all for runnin' you off pronto, not because he had anything against you, but because he could see settlers gettin' a toehold in his domain.

"Now one of our boys has been killed. Even Bishop might have trouble holdin' the boys back after that. I've talked to 'em, and they want the guilty man. They don't care about anybody else. What happens now is up to you."

"Not necessarily," Pagones objected. "We'll call a vote on it."

"You know how that'll go," Bannon objected. "Ten of you came in here with Mort Harper. Then he brought in Kies and Zapata. Now he's got other men. Supposin' you three vote to turn over the guilty man. How many others will vote that way? Cap may think right, but Cap will vote pretty much as Harper says. So will Purcell and Lamport. Anyway you look at it, the vote is going to be to fight rather than turn Zapata over."

"No way to be sure of that," Scatterfield objected. "Harper may decide to turn him over."

Bannon turned, his temper flaring. "Haven't you learned anything on this trip? Harper's using you. He brought you down here for his own reasons. He's out to steal Bishop's Valley from Hardy—that's what he wants. You're just a bunch of dupes!"

"You got any proof of that?" Crockett demanded.

"Only my eyes," Rock admitted, "but that's enough. He owns every one of you, lock, stock and barrel. I heard about that matter of you being in debt to Kies. Don't you suppose he planned all that?"

The door opened and Cap Mulholland came in, and with him was Collins. Cap's face flushed when he saw Rock.

"You'd better light out. If Pete Zapata sees you, he'll kill you."

"That might not be so easy," Bannon said sharply. "All men don't die easy, nor do they knuckle under to the first smooth talker who sells them a bill of goods."

Mulholland glared at him. "He promised us places, and we got 'em. Who's this Bishop to run us off? If it comes to war, then we'll fight."

"And die for Morton Harper? Do you think he'll let you keep what you have if he gets in control of this valley? He'll run you out of here without a penny. You're his excuse, that's all. If the law ever comes into this, he can always say that Bishop used violence to stop free American citizens from settling on the land."

"That's just what he's doin'," Cap said. "If he wants war he can have it!"

"Then I'd better go," Rock said. "I came here hopin' to make some peace talk. It looks like Zapata declared war for you. Now you've got to fight Mort Harper's war for him."

"You were one of us once," Pagones said. "You helped us on the trail. Why can't you help us now?"

Rock Bannon looked up, and his eyes hesitated on Sharon's face, then swept on. "Because you're on the wrong side," he said simply.

Sharon looked up and her eyes flashed. "But you were one of us," she protested. "You should be with us now. Don't you understand loyalty?"

"I was never one of you after Mort Harper came," he

said. Sharon flushed under his gaze. "Whatever I might have been, Harper took away from me. I ain't a smooth-talkin' man; guess I never rightly learned to say all I feel, but sometimes them that say little, feel a sight more."

He put one hand on the latch. "As for loyalty, my first loyalty's to Hardy Bishop," he said.

"But how could that be?" Sharon protested.

"He's my father," Rock said quietly, then he stepped quickly and silently out the door.

"His father!" Pagones stared after him. "Well, I'll be danged!"

"That don't cut any ice with me," Mulholland said. "Nor his talk. I got the place I want, and I aim to keep it. Harper says there ain't any way they can drive us off. He says we've got guns enough to hold our own, and this canyon ain't so easy to attack. I'm glad it's comin' to a showdown. We might as well get it over."

"All I want is to get to work," Collins said stubbornly. "I got a sight of it ahead, so if that Bishop aims to drive me off, I wish he'd come and get it over with."

"All that talk about Harper usin' us," Scatterfield said uneasily. "That didn't make sense!"

"Of course not!" Cap said hotly. "Bannon was against everything we tried to do, right from the start. He just never had no use for Mort Harper, that was all."

"Maybe there is something to what he says," Sharon interposed.

Cap glanced around irritably. "Beggin' your pardon, Sharon. This is man's talk."

"I'm not so sure," she flashed. "We women came across the plains with you. If we fight, my father may die; that makes it important to me. And if you think I'm going to stand by and let my home be turned into a shambles, you're wrong."

Her father started to speak, but she stepped forward. "Bannon said Harper was using you. Well, maybe he is and maybe he isn't, but there are a few things I'd like you to think about, because I've been thinking about them.

"Did Mort Harper look for this town site? No, he rode right to it, and to me that means he had planned it. What affair was it of his which trail we took? Yet he persuaded us, and we came down here. Who got us to stay? Harper! I'll admit I wanted to stay, and most of us did, but I'm wondering if he didn't count on that. And what about those wagons of supplies that turned up at just the right time?"

"Why, they just followed him on from the fort," Mulholland protested.

"Did they?" Sharon asked. "Go up and look at the trail. Mary and I looked at it, and no wagons have come over it since we did. Anyway, would he let those wagons come across that Indian country without more protection than they had? Those wagons were already here, waiting for us. They were back up in a canyon northeast of the trail."

"I don't believe that!" Collins said.

"Go look for yourselves then," Sharon said.

"You sound as if you're against us," Cap said. "Whose side are you on, anyway?"

"I'm on the side of the wagon train people, and you know it," she said. "But a lot of this doesn't look too good to me. The first day we were here I rode down in the valley with Mort, and he said something that had me wondering, something about taking it for himself."

"Don't make sense," Cap said stubbornly. "Anyway, womenfolks don't know about things like this."

Sharon was angry. In spite of herself, and knowing her anger only made Cap more stubborn, she said: "You didn't think there were any Indians, either. You took Mort's word for that. If it hadn't been for Bannon, we'd all have been killed."

She turned quickly and went out of the cabin. Swinging into the saddle, she started across toward her own cabin.

It was dark, and she could see the light in the saloon, and the lights in Collins's blacksmith shop, where his wife and little Davy would be waiting for him to return.

Angry, she paid little attention where she was going until suddenly a horseman loomed in the dark near her.

"Howdy!" he said, swinging alongside.

From his voice and bulk, she knew him at once as Hy Miller, a big teamster who sometimes served as relief bartender. He had been drinking.

She tried to push on, but he reached out and grabbed her wrist. "Don't be in no such hurry," he said, leering at her in the dimness. "I want to have a bit of palaver with you!"

"Well, I don't want to talk to you!" she said angrily. She tried to jerk her wrist away, but he only tightened his grip. Then he pulled her to him and slid his other arm around her waist. She struggled, and her mare sidestepped, pulling her from the saddle.

Miller dropped her, then slid from his own horse and grabbed her before she could escape. "I'll learn you a thing or two!" he said hoarsely. "It's about time you settlers were learnin' who's runnin' this shebang!"

What happened next, Sharon scarcely knew. She was suddenly wrenched from Miller's arms, and she heard a crack of a blow, and Miller went down into the grass.

"Run for the house!" It was Bannon's voice. "Quick!"

Miller came up with an oath, and she saw him charge. Bannon smashed his left into the big teamster's mouth and staggered him, but the man leaped in, swinging with both hands. There was no chance for science or skill. In the dimness the two men fought like animals, tooth and nail, yet Bannon kept slamming his right to the bigger man's stomach. The teamster coughed and gasped, and then Rock swung a right to his chin that staggered him, and followed it up with a right and a left. Miller went down, and Bannon stooped and grasped his shirt collar in his left hand.

Holding the man at arm's length in a throttling grip, Bannon smashed him in the face again and again, then he struck him in the body and hurled him to the ground. Sharon, wide-eyed and panting, still stood there. "Get to your house," Bannon snapped. "Tell your father to go armed, always. This is only the beginning!"

As she fled, somebody behind her said, "Hey, what's goin' on here?"

Behind her there was a pound of a horse's hoofs, and she knew Rock was gone. Swiftly, when she reached the house, she stripped the saddle from the mare and turned it into the corral. Then she went into the house and lighted the lamp. A few minutes later, her father came in. She told him all that had happened.

He stood there, resting his fists on the table. Then he straightened.

"Honey," he said, "I'm afraid I did wrong to stop here. I wish now I'd gone on with Bob Sprague and the others. They'd be most to Californy by now. I'm afraid—I'm afraid!"

V

Rock Bannon stopped that night in a line cabin six miles west of Poplar and across the valley. When morning came, he was just saddling up when Bat Chavez rode in. With him were Johnny Stark and Lew Murray. All three were armed.

Bat grinned at him. Then his eyes fell on the skinned knuckles, and he chuckled.

"Looks like you had some action."

"A little," Rock said, and then explained briefly. "You watch yourselves," he said, "and stick together. That outfit's out for trouble."

"All I want's a shot at Zapata," Bat said harshly. "I'll kill me a breed if I get it."

Rock mounted and rode north toward the ranch house. No act of his could avert trouble now. He had hoped to convince the settlers who came with the wagon train that they should break away from Mort Harper.

That would draw the lines plainly—the ranch against the land-grabbers. He knew that Mulholland was an honest, if a stupid man. The others of the train were honest, but some of them, like Purcell and Lamport, were firm adherents of Harper, and believed in him. This belief they combined with a dislike of Rock Bannon.

It had been a hard task to persuade Hardy Bishop to let them stay. The old man was a fire-eater, and he knew what it would mean to let settlers get a toehold in his rich valley. Once in, they would encroach more and more on his best range, until he was crowded back to nothing. Only his affection for Rock had convinced him—and the fact that he had gleaned from Rock's talk; among the settlers was a girl.

Rock Bannon knew what the old man was thinking. Lonely, hard-bitten and tough, Bishop was as affectionate

53

as many big bearlike men are. His heart was as big and warm as himself, and from the day he had taken Rock Bannon in, when the boy was orphaned at six when Kaw Indians had killed his parents, Bishop had lived as much for Rock as for his ranch. Now, more than anything, he wanted Rock settled, married, and living on the broad acres of Bishop's Valley.

It had been that as much as anything that brought him around to Rock's way of thinking when Rock planned to go east to Council Bluffs. Secretly, he hoped the boy would come back with a wife, and certainly there were no women around Bishop's Valley but an occasional squaw. He had never seen this girl with the wagon train, but he had gleaned more than a little from Rock's casual comments, and what he heard pleased him.

Hardy Bishop was a big man, weighing, now that he was heavy around the middle, nearly three hundred pounds. Yet in the days of his raw youth he tipped the beam at no less than two hundred and fifty pounds. On his hip even the big dragoon Colts looked insignificant, but he was scarcely less fast than Rock.

Seated deep in a cowhide-covered chair, he looked up when Rock came in, and grinned. He was just filling his pipe. There was a skinned place on Bannon's cheekbone, and his knuckles were raw.

"Trouble, you've had," Bishop said, his deep voice filling the room. "Been over to look at them settlers again? Think they killed Wes?"

"Not the settlers," Rock said. "One of the men with them."

Rock sat down on the butt of a log and quietly outlined the whole situation, explaining about Harper, Zapata, and the teamster.

"They had that stuff cached in the hills," Rock went on. "Red Lunney spotted it some time back. There were about a dozen men holed up back there with a lot of supplies, too many for themselves. He kept an eye on them, but they didn't wander around, and made no trouble, so he left them alone.

"Evidently Mort Harper had them planted there. The wagon train, as near as I can figure, he planned to use as a blind in case the government got into this. He could always say they were honest settlers looking for homes, and the government would be inclined to favor them. What he really wants is Bishop's Valley!"

"He'll have a time gettin' it!" Bishop said grimly. "I'll bank on that. I fit Indians all over these hills, but this valley I bought fair and square from old War Cloud. We never had no Indian trouble until lately, when the wagon trains started comin' through. Those Mormons, they had the right idea. Treat Indians good, pay for what you get, and no shootin' Indians for the fun of it, like some folks do!

"Why, Rock, I trapped all over these mountains. Lived with Indians, trapped with them, hunted with them, slept in their tepees. I never had trouble with them. I was through this country with Wilbur Price Hunt's Astorians when I was no more'n sixteen, but a man growed. I was with John Day in this country after that, and he saw more of it than any other man.

"Took me two years to drive these cattle in here. First ever seen in this country! I drove them up from Santa Fe in six or seven of the roughest drives any man ever saw, with Indians doin' most of my drivin' for me. They said I was crazy then, but now my cattle run these hills and they eat this valley grass until their sides are fit to bust. One of these days you'll start drivin' these cattle east. Mark my words, there'll come a day they'll make you rich. . . . And then some whippersnapper like this Harper— why!" He rubbed his jaw irritably, then looked up at Rock. "You see that girl? That Crockett girl?"

"Uh-huh," Rock admitted. "I did."

"Why not stop this here cayusin' around and bring

her home, son? Time you took a wife. Ain't no sense in
a man runnin' loose too long. I did, and then hadn't my
wife very long before she died. Fine girl, too."

"Hardy," Rock said suddenly, calling him by his first
name, as he had since Bishop first took him in hand as
a child, "I don't want war with those people. They're
askin' for it, and that Mulholland is simple enough to be
led by the nose by Harper. Why don't you let me go get
Zapata? I'll take him on myself. In fact," he added grimly,
"I'd like to! Then we can take some of the boys, get
Harper and his teamsters and start them out of here."

"Separate the sheep from the goats, eh?" Bishop
looked at him quizzically. "All right, son. I've gone along
with you this long. You take the boys, you get that Harper
out of there and start him back for Laramie.

"As for Zapata, do what you like. I've seen some men
with guns, and you're the fastest thing I ever did see, and
the best shot. But don't leave him alive. If I had my way,
we'd string every one of 'em to a poplar tree, and right
quick."

The old man grinned briefly at Bannon, leaned back
and lighted his pipe. So far as he was concerned, the sub-
ject was closed.

Bat Chavez was a man who made his own plans and
went his own way. Loyal to the greatest degree, he obeyed
Rock Bannon or Hardy Bishop without question. They
were his bosses, and he liked and respected them both.
However, he had another loyalty, and that was to the
memory of Wes Freeman.

He and Wes had ridden together, hunted together,
fought Indians together. Wes was younger, and Bat
Chavez had always considered himself the other's sponsor
as well as friend. Now Wes was dead, and to Bat Chavez
that opened a feud that could be settled only by blood.
Johnny Stark and Lew Murray were like-minded. Both
were young, hardy, and accustomed to live by the gun.

They understood men like Zapata. Of the three, perhaps the only one who rated anything like an even break with the half-breed was the half-Mexican, half-Irish Chavez. However, no one of them would have hesitated to draw on sight.

They weren't looking for trouble, but they were ready. In that frame of mind they started down the valley to move some of the cattle away from the mouth of Poplar Canyon. No one of them knew what he was riding into, and had they known, no one of them would have turned back. . . .

Mort Harper, in his living quarters in the back of the saloon, was disturbed. Things had not gone as he'd planned. Secure in his familiarity with men of Hardy Bishop's type, he had been positive that the arrival of the wagon train and the beginning of their settlement would precipitate trouble. He had counted on a sudden attack by Bishop, and perhaps the killing of one or more of the settlers. Nothing more, he knew, would have been required to unite them against the common enemy. Peaceloving they might be, but they were men of courage, and men who believed in independence and equal rights for all. Typically American, they wouldn't take any pushing around.

On his knowledge of their character and that of Bishop he had built his plans. Over a year before, he had seen Bishop's Valley, and the sight had aroused a lust for possession that he had never known could live within him. Since that day he had lived for but one thing: to possess Bishop's Valley, regardless of the cost.

It was beyond the reach of law. Few people in the country had any idea the valley existed or that it had been settled. His first thought was to ride in with a strong band of outlaws recruited from the border towns, and take the place by main force; but times, he knew, were changing.

Morton Harper was shrewd enough to understand that

the fight might arouse government inquiry. Fremont and Carson knew this country, and it was possible the Army might soon move into it. It would behoove him to have justice on his side.

The wagon trains offered that chance. From the first he had seen what a good chance it was. At the fort he watched them go through, and he saw the weariness of women and children, the haggard lines of men's faces. The novelty of the trip was over, and miles upon miles remained before they could reach Oregon. If he could get some of them into the valley country, he believed he could persuade them, by some method, to stay on. With that end in view, he watched until he saw the wagon train he wanted. Those which were led by able and positive men he had avoided. When he encountered Cap Mulholland, he was quick to perceive his opportunity.

In his visit to the camp he noted that Tom Crockett was a mild, tolerant man, friendly, and interested mainly in finding a new home and getting a plow into the ground. Pagones was a strong, able man, but not outspoken or likely to push himself into a position of leadership.

Pike Purcell and Lamport were honest, able men, but ignorant and alike in their dislike of Rock Bannon. Lamport, who was unmarried and thoroughly undesirable, had fancied himself for an inside track with Sharon Crockett until Bannon joined the train.

Rock Bannon was constantly with her, first as a wounded man needing care, and later as a rider. Lamport grew jealous. Purcell, married to a nagging wife, had looked after Sharon with desire. His own dislike of Bannon stemmed from the same source, but grew even more bitter because Pike sensed Bannon was the better man, and Pike hated him for it.

Mort Harper was quick to curry the favor of these two. He talked with them, flattered them subtly, and bought them drinks. He learned that Purcell was desperately hard up, and lent him some money. He gave Lamport a gun he admired.

The only flaw in the picture had been Rock Bannon, and in Rock, Harper was quick to recognize a formidable and dangerous antagonist. He also realized he had an excellent weapon in the veiled enmity of Purcell and Lamport.

His plans had gone ahead very well until the attack by Bishop failed to materialize. Despite himself, he was disturbed. Would the old man really let them settle there? He caused a few cattle to be killed for meat, and left evidence about. That Rock Bannon had found the remains of the slaughtered cattle and buried them, he could not know. The expected attack failed, and he sensed a falling away from him on the part of the settlers.

The only way he could hope to get the valley was by precipitating open warfare, killing off the Bishop forces, and taking possession. Then in due time he could eliminate the settlers themselves and reign supreme, possessor of one of the largest cattle empires in the country.

Pete Zapata was under no orders to kill, but the fact that he had killed Wes Freeman fell in line with Harper's plans. Yet he could sense the disaffection among the settlers. Crockett and Pagones could be a strong force against him, if they became stubborn. Something was needed to align them firmly on his side.

That chance came, as he had hoped it would come. With Pete Zapata, Hy Miller, Pike Purcell, Lamport and Collins, he was riding down into the valley when they saw Bat Chavez and the two Bishop riders approaching. Had Harper led his party along the trail where they had started, the paths of the two groups would not have intersected, but Harper reined in and waited.

Chavez wasn't the man to ride around trouble. In Lew Murray and Johnny Stark he had two companions who had never ridden around anything that even resembled trouble.

With guns loosened in holsters, they rode steadily on.

"Howdy!" Bat Chavez said. His eyes swung and fastened on Pete Zapata. "Where you ridin'?"

"Who's askin'?" Purcell demanded truculently. "We go where we want."

"Not on this range, you don't. You stick to your valley. This here's Bishop range."

"He own everything?" Miller demanded. "We ride where we please!"

"Looks like you been ridin' where somebody else pleased," Johnny Stark said, grinning. "In fact, that face looks like somebody rid all over you with spikes in his boots."

Miller's face flamed. -"There was three of 'em!" he snapped. "You couldn't do it. I think it's time we taught you Bishop riders a lesson, anyway."

"You mean," Chavez demanded insolently, "like that murderin' breed that shot Wes Freeman—in the back?"

Zapata's hand flashed for his gun, and Chavez was scarcely slower. Only the jerk of Zapata's horse's head saved him. As it was the horse took the bullet right through the head, and leaped straight up into the air, jerking Zapata's gun and spoiling his aim.

There was a sudden flurry of gunshots, and Mort Harper was quick to sense his chance. He drew his sixshooter and calmly shot Collins through the back.

The attack broke as quickly as it began. Zapata's horse had leaped, then hit the ground, stone dead. Thrown from the horse, Zapata lost his gun and sprawled in the grass, showing no desire to get up and join the fight or even hunt for his gun.

Outnumbered, and with Murray shot through the leg, the Bishop riders drew off. Purcell had been burned along the cheek, and Miller's horse was killed, so the battle ended after only a few seconds, with two horses and one man dead. In the excitement, only Mort Harper saw the flare of pained astonishment and accusation in Collins's eyes.

The blacksmith's mouth refused to shape words, and he died there in the grass. Harper looked down at him, a faint smile on his face. Collins had been a popular man, quiet and well liked. This would do what all Harper's other plans had failed to do.

"Collins got it?" Pike stood over him, his hard face saddened. "He was a good man." Of them all, Collins was the only man in the wagon train Pike Purcell had known before the trip began. They had come through the war together.

"Might's well bury him, I guess," Mort said.

Pike looked up. "No, we'll tote him back home. His widow'll want to see him. Reckon it'll go hard with her."

Mort Harper's lips thinned, but there was nothing he could say without arousing suspicion. Silently, the little cavalcade started back. Collins's body was tied to Pike's horse, and he walked alongside, trailed by Zapata and Miller.

For two days ominous quiet hung over the town of Poplar. Collins had been buried, and the faces of the settlers as they gathered about to see his body lowered into the grave proved to Harper how right he had been. No longer was there any doubt or hesitation. Now they were in the fight. He had walked back from that grave filled with triumph. Only a few days longer, and then he would begin the war in earnest.

Tom Crockett was a quiet man, but his face was stern and hard as he walked back home beside Sharon. "Well, we tried to avoid it, but now it's war," he said. "I think the sooner we have some action the better."

Sharon said nothing, but her heart was heavy within her. She no longer thought of Mort Harper. His glamour had faded, and always now, there was but one man in her thoughts, the tall, shy, hesitant Rock Bannon.

She always marveled that a man so hard, so sure of himself with men, horses or guns, could be so quiet and diffident with women. As a matter of fact, Rock Bannon had never seen any woman but an Indian squaw until he was eighteen years old, in Santa Fe.

Rock Bannon had never talked to a woman until he was twenty. Now he was twenty-seven, and he had probably talked to no more than six or seven white women or girls.

With deepening sadness and pain, she realized the killing of Collins had done all they had hoped to avoid. There would be war now, and knowing her father as she did, she knew the unrelenting stubbornness in him once he was resolved upon a course. She had seen him like this before. He always sought to avoid trouble, always saw the best in people, yet when the battle line was laid down, no man would stay there longer than Tom Crockett.

Only one man was silent on the walk back from the grave. Dud Kitchen, weak and pale from his own narrow escape, was out for the first time. He was very tired, and he was glad when he was back in the Pagones' house and could lie down and rest. He was up too soon, he knew, but Collins had been his friend. Now, lying alone in the gathering darkness and hearing the low mutter of men's voices in the other room, he was sorry he had gone.

He had gone over to the Collins house to see his old friend once before he was buried, and he was there when the widow and Scatterfield had dressed him in his Sunday-go-to-meeting clothes. He saw something then that filled the whole inside of him with horror. He saw what none of them seemed to have noticed, that Collins had been shot in back! Yet he had seen something more than that, and it was that thing that disturbed him.

Dud Kitchen was a friendly, cheerful young man who liked nothing better than to sing and play the mandolin. Yet in his life, from Missouri to Texas, he had more than a little experience with guns. Once, too, he had gone down the river to New Orleans, and he had learned many things on that trip.

Among other things he knew the dragoon Colt had the impact of an ax and would blow a hole in a man big enough to run a buffalo through, or so it was phrased on the frontier. The hole in Collins had been much smaller at the point of entry; it had been wide and ugly at the point of exit.

Opening the door between the living room-kitchen of the Pagones' house, Pike walked in to look at Dud. "Better get yourself well, Dud," Pike said. "We'll need all hands for this fuss."

"Was it bad, Pike?" Kitchen asked. His voice was faint, and in the dim light Pike could not see what lay in the younger man's eyes.

"No, I figure it wasn't so bad," Pike said. "Only a few shots fired. It was over so quick I scarce got my gun out. That Bat Chavez, him and Zapata were fastest, but Pete's horse swung around and spoiled his aim for him. Guess it saved his life, though, cause Bat's bullet hit the horse right in the head. Between the eyes.

"The horse rared up and throwed Pete, and I jumped my horse away to keep from gettin' in a tangle. Lamport, he scored a shot on one of them other fellows. We seen him jerk and seen the blood on him as they were ridin' off."

Dud Kitchen waited a long moment, then he said carefully: "Who killed Collins?"

Purcell seemed to scowl. "Don't rightly know. There was a sight of shootin' goin' on. Might have been any one of them three. Don't you worry about that. We'll get all three of them, so we won't miss gettin' the right one."

"Have they got good guns?" Dud asked. "I'll bet they have!"

"Same as us. Dragoon Colts. One of 'em had an old Walker, though. Big gun, too. Shoots like a rifle."

After Pike Purcell had gone Dud Kitchen lay alone in

the dark room, thinking. His thought frightened him, and yet, he was himself down from a shot by Zapata, who was on their own side. Collins had been shot in the back.

Whatever he had been shot by, Dud Kitchen was willing to take an oath it had been neither a Walker nor a Dragoon Colt. The hole was much smaller. The chest of the man had been frightfully torn. Sometimes men cut their bullets off flat across the nose to make them kill better. Dud had seen that done. It usually tore a man up pretty bad.

VI

J OHNNY STARK brought the news of the fight to Rock Bannon. He was with Bishop at the time, and the old man's face hardened.

"Well, there it is, Rock! We can't give them any more time now. They've had their chance, and from now on she'll be open warfare." Bishop looked up at Stark. "Take six men back with you. Have Monty go with the buckboard and bring Lew here to the ranch house, where he can have proper care. You tell Red I want to see him, but he'll be in charge when he goes back."

Rock got up and paced the floor. He ran his fingers through his shock of black, curly hair. His face was stern and hard. He knew what this meant. One man had gone down, Johnny said. From his description of the man it would be Collins, one of the good men. That would serve to unite the settlers in a compact lot. Despite all his desires to avoid trouble, they were in for it now, and it would be a case of dog eat dog. What would Sharon think of all this?

Hastily, he computed the numbers at the townsite. Their numbers were still slightly inferior to those on the Bishop ranch, but due to expected Indian trouble and the stock, many of the Bishop hands must remain on the far ranges.

"I'm going out," he said at last. "I'm going down to Poplar. Also, I'm going to have a look in that canyon where Harper's stuff was cached."

"You watch yourself, boy!" Bishop said. He heaved himself up in his chair. "You take care! I'm figurin' on you havin' this ranch, and I ain't wantin' to will it to no corpse."

Rock hurried down to the corral and saw Johnny Stark leading out the steel-dust, all saddled and ready.

"I figured you'd be ridin', Rock," he said grimly. He

handed the reins to him and started to turn away, then he stepped back.

"Rock," he said, "somethin' I been goin' to tell somebody. I forgot to mention it back there. Rock, I don't think any of us killed Collins!"

Bannon wheeled and grabbed the cowhand by the arm. His eyes were like steel.

"What do you mean? Give it to me, quick!"

"Hey!" Johnny said. "Ease up on that arm!" He grinned. "You got a grip like a bear trap." He rubbed his arm. "Why, I been thinkin' about that ever since. Bat was thinkin' only of Zapata. I shot at that Miller, the guy you whipped. I got his horse. Lew, he burned that long lean mountain man along the cheek, tryin' for a head shot. Actually, this here Collins hombre was off to our left. None of us shot that way."

"You're sure about that?" Bannon demanded.

His mind was working swiftly. If one thing would arouse anger against Bishop among the settlers, it would be the killing of one of their own number, and particularly one so well liked as Collins had been.

Bannon stared at the rider. "Did you see anybody near him? Who was over at that side?"

"This here Collins hombre who got shot was in the front rank," Johnny said. "Then there was a heavy-set, sandy sort of guy with a beard, and a tall hombre in a white hat with a dark coat."

The bearded man would be Lamport, the man in the white hat was Mort Harper.

Rock Bannon swung a leg over the saddle. "Johnny, you tell Red to sit tight," he said. "I'm riding to Poplar."

"Want me along?" Stark asked eagerly. "You better take some help. Those hombres are killin' now. They're in a sweat, all of them."

Rock shook his head. "No, I'll go alone," he said. "Tell Red to wait at the cabin."

Rock wheeled the gray and cut across the valley. There

was still a chance to avoid a battle if he could get to Poplar in time, yet he had a feeling that Harper would not wait. Hostilities had begun, and that was what he had been playing for all the time. Now he had his excuse to wipe out the Bishop forces, and he would be quick to take advantage of it.

Yet before he was halfway down the valley, he reined in on the slope of a low hill. Miles to the south he could see a group of horsemen cutting across toward the line cabin. Bat Chavez was there, alone with the wounded Murray.

Red would be starting soon, but would get there too late to help Bat or Murray. Within a matter of half an hour they would be attacking. From where he was it would take him all of that time and probably more to reach them. There was no time to go back. Wheeling the stallion, he started down the valley, angling away from the group of riders.

In the distance, around the peaks towering against the sky, dark clouds were banking. A jagged streak of lightning ripped the horizon to shreds of flame, then vanished, and there was a distant roll of thunder, muttering among the dark and distant ravines like the echoes of distant battle.

The gray horse ran through the tall grass, sweeping around groves of aspen and alder, keeping to the low ground. He splashed through a swale, crested a long, low hill that cut athwart the valley, and turned at right angles down the draw toward the cover of the far-off trees. The cool wind whipped against his face, and he felt a breath of moist wind as it shifted, feeling for the course of the storm.

The big horse was running smoothly, liking the feel of running, as he always did, letting his powerful muscles out and stretching them. Leaning forward to break the wind and let the weight of his body help the running horse, Rock Bannon talked, speaking softly to the stallion. He knew it loved his voice, for between the horse and man there was that companionship and understanding that come between a man and horse only when they have known many trails together, have shared the water of the same creeks, and run over long swells of prairie as they were running now.

Yet then he heard the distant sound of a rifle, and then a roll of shots.

"Bat, I hope to heaven you're under cover!" he muttered. "I hope they didn't surprise you!"

He eased the horse's running now, because he might rush upon some of them sooner than he expected. He slid his rifle from the scabbard and raced into the trees. The sound of firing was nearer now. He slowed the horse to a walk, letting him take a blow, his eyes searching the brush. There was still some distance to go, but there was firing, and that meant that Bat was under cover. They had not caught him flatfooted, at least.

He swung the horse up into the rocks and slid from the saddle, easing forward to the rim of the shelf overhanging the line cabin. Lying face down among the rocks, he could see puffs of smoke from the brush around the cabin. Waiting until he saw a gleam of light on a rifle, he fired.

Almost instantly, a man some distance away leaped up and started to run for a boulder. Swinging the rifle, Rock snapped a shot at him and the man went to his knees, then started to crawl for shelter.

A rifle bellowed down below and a shot glanced off a rock, kicking splinters into Bannon's face. He eased back and worked down the slope a bit, studying the situation below. One man at least was wounded.

Suddenly, a horseman leaped a horse from behind some trees, and, dragging a flaming mass of brush, raced toward the cabin. It was a foolhardy thing to do, but instantly, Bannon saw his purpose, for the rifle fire had attracted Bat Chavez to the other side of the cabin. Rock lifted his own rifle and steadied it. A flashing instant of aim, then he fired.

The horseman threw up his arms and toppled back off the horse, right into the mass of flaming brush. He screamed once, horribly, then rolled clear, fighting the fire in his garments and dragging himself in the dust. Another man rushed from the brush to aid him, and Rock held his fire.

Suddenly, there was a heavy roll of thunder. Looking around, he saw the clouds had come nearer, and now there was a sprinkle of rain. At the same instant he heard the pounding of horses' hoofs. Snapping a quick shot at the brush, he was in time to hear a startled yell and then the attackers broke from the brush and, scrambling to their saddles, charged away across the valley, and then the rain broke with a thundering roar, a veritable cloudburst.

Rushing to the gray, he swung into the saddle and put the animal around to a steep slide of shale, and rode down to the barn near the corral. Johnny rushed up to him.

"You all right?"

"Yeah. How's Bat?"

"Don't know. Bat went in. You go ahead. I'll fix your horse up."

Rock sprinted for the house and got in, slamming the door after him. Bat looked around, grinning widely.

"Man, was I glad to hear that rifle of yours!" he said. "They had me surrounded. Lew wanted to get into it, but I was afraid his wound would open and start bleedin' again. Well, we drove 'em off."

"You get anybody?"

"Scratched a couple. Maybe got one. You got one that first shot. I seen him fall. That'll be one down and two bad hurt, maybe four. Looks like we come out of that on top."

"I was headed for Poplar and saw them. I was afraid you'd be outside and they'd split up on you."

Chavez spat. "They mighty near did. I'd just been to the spring for water."

Rock stared into the fire. This would mean nothing one

way or another. They had been turned back from the first attack, but they would not be convinced. He had killed a man, and who it was would matter a great deal, he knew. Certainly if it was another of the settlers he would have small chance of selling them on quitting.

Yet he was just as resolved now as before the attack. This thing must be stopped. It was never too late to try. The rain was roaring upon the roof, a full-fledged cloudburst. They would never expect him in a flood like that. They would be inside, and expecting everyone else to be there, too. If he circled around and came down the canyon, it would be the best chance. If they were keeping watch at all, it would be from this direction. . . .

Sharon was outside when she saw the rain coming, and she waited for it, liking the cool air. Over the distant mountains across the valley there were vivid streaks of lightning. It was already storming there, and a frightful storm by all appearances.

She was alone, and glad of it. Mary had wanted her to come to the Collins house, where several of the women had gathered, but she knew she could never stand to be cooped up now. She was restless and worried. Her father was out there, and for all his courage and willingness to go, Tom Crockett was no fighting man. He was not like Bannon.

Strangely, now, she was little worried about Rock Bannon. He was hard, seemingly impervious to harm. Even now he might be over there across the valley. He might be killing her father, or her father might be shooting him. Twelve men had ridden away. Eight of them were settlers. Collins was dead and Dud Kitchen still too weak to ride, but the others had gone to a man. Mulholland, Satterfield, Pagones, Lamport, Purcell, Olsen and Greene. And, of course, her father.

Then the rain came. A scattering of big drops, then the rolling wall of it. She turned and went inside. There were a few places where the roof was not too tight. She put pans under them, and lighted a light which she put on the table near the window. Her father's leg was still not too strong, and it worried her to think he was out there in all this.

She caught a glimpse of herself in the mirror, a tall girl with a great mass of red-gold hair done in two thick braids about her head, her face too pale, her eyes too large.

She heard them coming before she saw them, and saw a horseman break away from the others and cross the grass, now worn thin from much travel. When the horse was stabled her father came in, stamping his feet and slipping out of the slicker. His gray hat was black with rain, and she took it close to the fire. The coffee was ready, and she poured a cup, then went for a bowl to get some soup for him.

He sat down at the table—sat down as suddenly as if his legs had been cut off, and she noticed with a sudden qualm that he looked old, tired. His eyes lifted to hers and he smiled wanly.

"Guess I'm no fighting man, Sharon," he said. "I just wasn't cut out for it. When that man fell into the flames today, I nearly wilted."

"Who was it?" she asked quickly. "One of our men?"

"No, it was a teamster. One of the bunch that hangs around the saloon. His name was Osburn. We rushed the house, and one of the men inside opened fire. Wounded one of the men, first shot. We had the house surrounded, though, and would have had them in a few minutes; but then someone opened up on us from the cliff.

"It was Bannon, I'm sure of that. He killed Hy Miller. Got him with his first shot, although how he saw him I can't imagine. Then he wounded Satterfield. Shot him through the leg, about like I was. This Osburn got on a horse, and—" His voice rambled on, and all she could think about was that her father was home, that her father was safe.

When his voice died away and he was eating the hot soup, she said, "And Bannon? Was he hurt?"

"No, he wasn't hurt. He never seems to get hurt. He's a hard man, Sharon."

"But a good man, Father!" she said suddenly. "He's a good man. Oh, I wish things were different!"

"Don't think it, Sharon," her father said, shaking his head. "He's not for you. He's a wild, ruthless man. A man who lives by the gun. Collins is dead, and by one of this man's friends, and they'll never let up now, nor will we. It's a war to the end."

"But why, Father? Why?" Sharon's voice broke. "Oh, when I think that we might have gone by the other trail! We might have been in Oregon now. Sometimes I believe that everything Bannon ever said about Mort Harper was true. All we've done is to come on here into this trap, and now our oxen are gone, all but the two you use to plow, and we're in debt."

"I know." Crockett stirred restlessly. "But it might have been as bad wherever we went. You must understand that. We may be mistaken in Mort. He's done what he could, and he's standing by us in this fight."

The fire flickered and hissed with the falling drops of rain in the chimney, and Sharon crossed and knelt beside the fire, liking the warm feel of it on her knees. She sat there, staring into the flames, hearing the unrelenting thunder of the rain and wondering where he was.

Where would it all end? That boy, Wes Freeman, slain in the hills. Then Collins, and now Miller. Dud Kitchen recovering from a wound. Jim Satterfield down, and the whole affair only beginning and no end in sight. The door opened suddenly and without warning, and she whirled, coming to her feet with her eyes wide.

Disappointment swept over her, and then fear. Pete Zapata was closing the door after him. He was smiling at her, his queer, flat face wet with rain, his narrow rattler's eyes searching the corners of the room.

"Not here?" he whispered hoarsely. "Purty soon, mebbe."

"Who—who do you mean?" she gasped.

Her father was sitting up very straight, his eyes on the half-breed. Zapata glanced at him with thinly veiled contempt, then shrugged.

"Who? That Rock Bannon. A few minutes ago he comes down the canyon on hees horse; now he ees here somewhere. Who knows? But soon he weel come here, and then—" He smiled, showing his yellow teeth between thick lips. His eyes shifted from her to her father. "Eeef one speaks to warn heem, I keel the other one, you see? Huh?"

Fear left her lips stiff, her eyes wide. Slowly, she turned back to the fire. Bannon would come here; Zapata was right. If Rock had come again to Poplar he would not leave without seeing her. He might come at any minute. She must think, she must somehow contrive to warn him.

The steel-dust stallion liked the dim, shallow cave in which Rock stopped him, but he didn't like being left alone. He whimpered a little, and snorted with fear as Bannon started to move away, but when Rock spoke, the stallion quieted, resigned to what was to come.

Rock Bannon moved out swiftly, keeping under the trees but working his way closer and closer to the house of Pagones. He didn't know what he was getting into, but Pagones was the most reliable of them all, and the strongest one. If resistance to Harper was to come, it must come from him. Crockett lacked the force of character, even though he might have the will. Besides, Pagones had the knowledge, very close to him, that one of Harper's men had shot down Dud Kitchen.

Pagones hadn't chosen his son-in-law. Mary had done that for herself, but Pagones couldn't have found anyone he liked better. Dud was energetic, tireless, capable and full of good humor. George Pagones, in his heart, had never felt sure of Mort Harper. He had listened with one part of his mind to Bannon's protests, even while the smooth words of Harper beguiled him.

Pagones had returned wet and tired. Like Crockett, he had no love of killing. He had seen Osburn tumble into the flames, he had seen Miller killed. Knowing the trouble Miller had caused, and how he had attacked Sharon while drunk, Pagones was not sorry to see him die. If it had to be someone, it might as well have been Miller. Yet seeing any man die is a shock, and he had been close to the man.

Many men are aggressive and willing enough to fight, but when they see death strike suddenly and horribly their courage oozes away. Pagones had the courage to defend himself, but his heart was not in this fight, and the action of the day had served to make him very thoughtful.

Something was worrying Dud Kitchen. He had been noticing that for several days, yet there had been no chance to talk to him when the womenfolks were not around. He felt the need of talking to him now, and got up and went into the room. He was there, beside the bed, when a breath of cold air struck him and he heard a startled gasp from his wife.

Gun in hand, he stepped back to the door. Rock Bannon was closing it after him. He turned now, and looked at the gun in Pagones' hand. Bannon smiled grimly.

"Well, you've got the drop on me, Pag. What happens now?"

"What do you want here?" Pagones demanded sternly. "Don't you know that if you keep coming back they'll kill you?"

"Just so it isn't you, Pag," Bannon said. "I always reckoned you a friend."

Pagones holstered his gun. "Come in," he said. "I take it you've come to talk."

Mary and her mother stood facing him, their eyes shining with apprehension. There was a scuffling of feet from the other room, and Dud Kitchen was in the door.

"Howdy," he said. "They'll kill you, Rock. I heard Zapata say he was after you. He said he was going to get you next."

"All right." Rock dropped into a chair, his right-hand holster in his lap, the ivory gun butt near his right hand. His dark-blue shirt was open at the neck, his leather jacket unbuttoned. The candle and firelight flickered on the bright butts of the cartridges in his twin belts.

Dud's face was very pale, but somehow Rock sensed that Dud was glad to see him, and it made him feel better, and made the talk come easier. Pagones' cheekbones glistened in the firelight, and his eyes were steady on Bannon's face as he waited for him to begin. It was very still in the room. A drop of water fell into the fire and hissed itself into extinction.

Mary stooped, her freckles dark against the pallor of her face, and dropped a handful of small sticks on the fire.

"Pag," Bannon began slowly, "I've never wanted this fight. I don't think you have. I don't think Crockett did either, or Dud here. There's no use me tryin' to talk to Tom. He's a good man, and he knows what he wants, but he hasn't force enough to make it stick. He couldn't stand against Harper. There's only one man here can do that, Pagones, and that's you."

"Harper's my friend," Pagones said evenly. "He led us here. This is his fight and ours."

"You don't believe that," Rock said. "Not down inside, you don't. Collins's death brought you into it. That made it your fight and Crockett's fight. The truth is all you men want is homes. That's what your wife wants, and Mary. That's what Sharon wants, too. That's what Cap wants, and the rest of them.

"What Mort Harper wants is land and power. He intends to have them, no matter who dies, or when. I've been here before to try to stop this trouble. I'm here again, now.

"One of our men died first, and he was a good boy.

He was murdered, Pagones, murdered as no man in the wagon train would kill any man, not even an Indian. Purcell didn't like me. Neither did Lamport. Cap was your leader, but he listened too readily to that glib tongue of Harper's."

"We all did," Dud said. "I listened, too. I listened for a while, anyway."

Mary moved up behind his chair and put her hand on his shoulder. He looked up quickly, and she smiled.

"Get to the point!" Pagones said. All that Bannon said was true. He knew it as well as Rock. He had listened to Harper, but secretly he had always been afraid that Bannon was right. He had been afraid of this trail. There might be a way out yet, but it had to be a way. They had no oxen now, they had no money. They were here, and they could not escape.

Rock leaned a hand on his knee. "Pagones, my boys say they didn't kill Collins!"

Dud Kitchen drew in his breath, and Mary looked at him in sudden apprehension.

"What's that you say?" Pagones demanded.

"I repeat, I talked to my boys, and they say they didn't kill Collins. Bat Chavez couldn't see anything but Zapata, Stark and Murray weren't even facing toward Collins then. They say they didn't kill him."

"There was a lot of shooting," Pagones said. "Anything might of happened."

"That's right," Bannon agreed. "But my boys don't think they shot Collins, and that leaves a big question."

"It doesn't leave no question for me!" Dud flared suddenly. "I saw that wound of Collins's! He was shot in the back!"

Pagones' face hardened. He stared down at the floor, his jaw muscles working. Was nothing ever simple any more? Was there nothing on which a man could depend? How had he got into this mess, anyway. What should he do?

"Who do you think?" he asked. "You mean Zapata?"

Their eyes were all on Rock Bannon, waiting, tense. "No," he said. "I mean Mort Harper!" He got up and moved restlessly around the room.

"But that's crazy!" Pagones leaped to his feet. "What would be the object? Is there any reason why he would kill a man on his own side?"

"You know the answer to that as well as I," Bannon said. He got up, too. "He wanted you in this fight, and that was the only way he could get you in. Purcell and Lamport were fire-eaters. They were in, but they weren't enough. He wanted the rest of you, the good, sober, industrious citizens, the men whose reputations at home were good, the men who would look honest to the military if they ever came west."

"I saw that wound," Kitchen repeated. "Collins was killed with a small gun, a small gun with flat-nose or split-ended bullets."

"Who has such a gun?" Pagones said. "You all know that Harper carries a Dragoon, like the rest of us."

"In sight, he does," Bannon agreed. "Mort Harper may pack another one."

Rock stopped, feet wide apart. "I've got to get out of here, Pag. I've got to get going, and fast. There's not much chance of anybody being out tonight, but I can't gamble on that. I've got to get away from here, but this is the last time I'll come. I've tried to tell you about Mort Harper for a long time. You've got your last chance to break away, because I'm telling you that if you don't break away there won't be a building standing on this ground within forty-eight hours."

Pagones' head jerked up. "Is that an ultimatum?"

"You bet it is!" Bannon snapped. "If I'd let Bishop have his head, you'd have all been out of here long ago. Wes would be alive now, and Collins, and Murray wouldn't be packin' that slug in his leg, and Dud would be on his feet. If I'd not kept Bishop off you, he would have faced you with forty armed men and ordered you off before you had a stake down or a foundation laid.

"Those boys of ours are spoilin' for a fight. They hate Harper's innards, and they want Zapata. He's a murderin' outlaw, and they all know it."

"I don't know that I can do anything," Pagones protested. "We have to think of Zapata as it is. Harper's the only thing that keeps him and those teamsters off our places and away from our women, anyway!"

Rock Bannon started for the door. With his hand on the latch, he turned, sliding into his slicker.

"You step aside and there won't be any Zapata or his friends!" he declared. "We'll wipe them out so fast they'll be only a memory. We just don't want to kill good people. You can keep your places. We let you come in, and we'll let you stay."

He turned and slipped out the door into the rain. For an instant, he hesitated, letting his eyes grow accustomed to the dark. Rain fell in slanting sheets, striking his face like hailstones and rattling against his oilskin slicker like on a tin roof. Water stood in puddles on the ground and when he stepped down a large drop fell from a tree down the back of his neck.

He hesitated, close against the wet tree trunk, and stared into the night. There was a glow of light from the window of the Crockett place. Somebody was still up. He hesitated, knowing it was dangerous to remain longer, yet longing for a sight of Sharon, for the chance to take her in his arms.

He never had. He had never kissed her, never held her hand. It was all a matter of their eyes, and yet he felt she understood, and perhaps responded to his feeling.

There were lights from the saloon. They would all be down there now, playing cards, drinking. It was a pity he had none of the boys here. They could go in and wipe them out in one final, desperate battle. Lightning flashed, and revealed the stark wet outlines of the buildings, the green of the grass, worn down now, between him and the Crockett cabin.

He stepped out from the tree and started across the open, hearing the far-off thunder muttering among the peaks of the mountains beyond the valley, muttering among the cliffs and boulders like a disgruntled man in his sleep.

He did not fasten his slicker, but held it together with his left hand and kept his right in his pocket, slopping across the wet ground with the rain battering the brim of his hat, beating with angry, skeleton fingers against the slicker.

Under the trees, he hesitated, watching the house. There was no horse around. Suddenly, a column of sparks went up from the chimney as if someone had thrown some sticks on the fire. He started to move, and another cluster of sparks went up. He hesitated, a signal? But who would know he was near?

A third time. Three times was a warning, three smokes, three rifle shots—what could it be? Who could know he was here? It was nonsense, of course, but the sparks made him feel uneasy.

Then again, three times, once very weakly, sparks mounted from the chimney. Somebody was playing with the fire, tapping with a stick on the burning wood, or stirring the fire.

No matter. He was going in. He felt cold, and the warmth of the room would be good again before he began his long ride to the line cabin. A long ride because it would be foolhardy to go down the canyon toward the valley.

He stepped out from under the tree and walked up to the house. His boots made sucking noises in the mud before the door. Lightning flashed and the water glistened on the smooth boards of the door. He should knock, but he stepped up and, keeping to the left of the door, he reached across with his left hand and drew the door wide.

A gun blasted, and he saw the sudden dart of fire from the darkness by the fireplace. The bullet smashed into the door, and then he went in with a rush.

He caught a glimpse of Sharon, her eyes wide with fright, scrambling away from the fire. Zapata lunged from the shadows, his face set in a snarl of bared teeth and gleaming eyes. His gun blasted again, and a bullet snatched at Rock's jacket. Bannon thumbed his gun.

Zapata staggered as though struck by a blow in the stomach. As Rock started for him, he leaped for an inner door. Rock lunged after him, firing again, and there was a crash as he went through the sack-covered window.

Wheeling, Rock leaped for the door and went out. Zapata's gun barked, and something laid a white-hot iron across his leg. Rock brought his gun up and turned his right side to the crouching man, and fired again, fired as though on a target range.

The half-breed coughed, and his pistol dropped into the mud. He clawed with agonized fingers at the other gun, and Rock Bannon could see the front of his shirt darkening with pounding rain and blood, and then Bannon fired again, and the breed went down, clawing at the mud.

A door slammed and there was a yell. Rock wheeled and saw Sharon in the doorway. "I can't stop," he said. "Talk to Pagones." And even as he spoke, he was running across the worn grass toward the trees.

A rifle barked, then another, and then intermittent shots. Crying with fear for him, Sharon Crockett stood in the door, staring into the darkness. Lightning flared, and through the slanting rain she caught a brief glimpse of him, a rifle flared, and then he was gone into the trees. A moment later they heard the pounding of hoofs.

"They'll never catch him on that horse," Tom Crockett said. "He got away!" Sharon turned, and her father was smiling. "Yes, daughter, I'm glad he got away. I'm glad he killed that murderer."

"Oh, Father!" Then his arms were around her, and as

running feet slapped in the mud outside, he pushed the door shut.

The door slammed open, and Mort Harper shoved into the room. Behind him were four men, their faces hard, their guns ready.

"What was he doing here?" Harper demanded. "That man's a killer! He's our enemy. Why should he come here?"

"I don't know why he came!" Crockett said coldly. "He never had a chance to say. Zapata had been waiting for him all evening. He seemed to believe he would be here. When Bannon came in, he fired and missed. He won't miss again."

Harper stared at him, his face livid and angry under the glistening dampness of the rain.

"You seem glad!" he cried.

"I am!" Crockett said. "That Zapata was a killer, and he deserved killing."

"And I'm glad," Sharon said, her chin lifted. "I'm glad Bannon killed him, glad that Bannon got away."

There was an angry mutter from the men behind Harper, but Mort put up a restraining hand. "This sounds like rebellion. Well, we'll have none of that in this camp. I've been patient with you, Sharon, but my patience is wearing thin."

"Who cares about your patience?" Anger rose in Sharon's eyes. "Your soft talk and lies won't convince us any longer. We want our oxen back, tomorrow! We've had enough of this. We'll get out of here tomorrow if we have to walk."

"No you won't," Harper said. "Come on, boys. We'll go now."

"Let's teach 'em a lesson, boss," one man said angrily. "To blazes with this palaver!"

"Not now," Harper said. His nostrils were flared with anger, and his face was hard. "Later!"

When the door closed after them, Tom Crockett's face

was white. "Well, Sharon," he said quietly, "for better or worse, there it is. Tomorrow we may have to fight. Your mother helped me fight Indians once, long ago. Could you?"

Sharon turned, and suddenly she smiled. "Do you need to ask?"

"No," he smiled back, and she could see a new light in his eyes, almost as if the killing of Zapata and the statement to Harper had made him younger, stronger. "No, I don't," he repeated. "You'd better get some sleep. I'm going to clean my rifle."

VII

ROCK BANNON's steel-dust stallion took the trail up the canyon at a rapid clip. They might follow him, Bannon knew, and he needed all the lead he could get. Some of those men had been in these hills for quite some time, yet if he ever got away into the wilderness around Day's River, they would never find him.

Shooting it out with six or seven killers was no part of his plan, and he knew the teamsters who had come to Poplar were just that, a band of renegades recruited from the scourings of the wagon trains passing through the fort. After the immediate dash, however, he slowed down to give the steel-dust better footing.

He turned northeast when he came out of Poplar Canyon and rode down into a deep draw that ended in a meadow. The bottom of the draw was roaring with water that had run off the mountain, but as yet it was no more than a foot deep. Far below he could hear the thunder of Day's River, roaring at full flood now.

The canyon through the Narrows would be a ghastly sight with its weight of thundering white water. Always a turmoil, now it would be doubled and tripled by the cloudburst. Rain slanted down, pouring unceasingly on the hills.

The trail by which he had come would be useless on his return. By now the water would be too deep in the narrow canyon up which he had ridden. He must find a new trail, a way to cut back from the primitive wilderness into which he was riding, and down through the valley where Freeman had been killed, and then through the mountains.

Briefly, he halted the big stallion in the lee of a jutting shoulder of granite where wind and rain were cast off into the flat of the valley. Knowing his horse would need every ounce of its strength he swung down, and his shoulder against the rock, he studied the situation in his mind's eye.

His first desperate flight had taken him northwest into the wild country. Had he headed south he must soon have come out on the plains beyond the entrance to Bishop's Valley where he would have nothing but the speed of his own horse to assist his escape.

He was needed here, now. Any flight was temporary, so in turning north he had kept himself within striking distance of the enemy. His problem now was to find a way through the rugged mountain barrier, towering thousands of feet above him, into Bishop's Valley, and across the valley to home.

No man knew these mountains well, but Hardy Bishop knew them better than anyone else. Next to him, Rock himself knew them best, but with all his knowledge they presented a weird and unbelievable tangle of ridges, canyons, jagged crests, peaks and chasms. At the upper end of the valley the stream roared down a gorge often three thousand feet deep, and with only the thinnest of trails along the cliffs of the Narrows.

The isolated valley might have been walled for the express purpose of keeping him out, for as he ran over the possible routes into the valley, one by one he had to forget them. Bailey's Creek would be a thundering torrent now, water roaring eight to ten feet deep in the narrow canyon. Trapper's Gulch would be no better, and the only other two routes would be equally impassable.

Rock stared at the dark bulk of the mountain through the slanting rain. He stared at it, but could see nothing but Stygian darkness. Every branch, every rivulet, every stream would be a roaring cataract now. If there were a route into the valley now, it must be over the ridge. The very thought made him swallow and turn chill. He knew what those ridges and peaks were in quiet hours. They could be traveled, and he had traveled them, but only when he could see and feel his way along. Now, with lightning crashing, thunder butting against the cliffs, and clouds gathered around them, it would be an awesome inferno of lightning and granite, a place for no living thing.

But the thought in the back of his mind kept returning. Hardy Bishop was alone, or practically so. He had sent Red to the line cabin nearest Harper with most of the fighting men. Others were in a cabin near the Narrows, and miles away. Only two men would be at home besides the cook.

Rock Bannon did not make the mistake of underestimating his enemy. Mort Harper had planned this foray with care. He would not have begun without a careful study of the forces to be arrayed against him. He would know how many men were at the line cabin, and the result of his figuring must certainly be to convince him that the ranch house was alone, and Hardy Bishop, the heart, soul and brain of the Bishop strength, was there.

There was a route over the mountain. Once, by day, Bannon had traveled it. He must skirt a canyon hundreds of feet deep along a path that clung like an eyebrow to the sheer face of the cliff. He must ride across the long swelling slope of the mountain among trees and boulders, then between two peaks, and angle through the forest down the opposite side.

At best it was a twelve-mile ride, and might stretch that a bit. Even by day it was dangerous and slow going. And he needed only his own eyes to convince him that lightning was making a playground of the hillside now.

"All right, boy," he said gently to the horse. "You aren't going to like this, but neither am I." He swung into saddle and moved out into the wind.

As he breasted the shoulder of granite, the wind struck him like a solid wall, and the rain lashed at his garments, plucking at the fastenings of his oilskin. He turned the horse down the canyon that would take them to the cliff face across which he must ride. He preferred not to think of that.

Drawing near, the canyon walls began to close in upon him until it became a giant chute down which the water thundered in a mighty Niagara of sound. Great masses of water churned in an enormous maelstrom below and the steel-dust stallion snorted and shied from its roaring.

Rock spoke to the horse and touched it on the shoulder. Reassured, it felt gingerly for the path, and moved out. A spout of water gushing from some crack in the rock struck him like a blow, drenching him anew and making the stallion jump. He steadied the horse with a tight rein, then relaxed and let the horse have his head. He could see absolutely nothing ahead of him.

Thunder and the rolling of gigantic boulders reverberated down the rock walled canyon, and occasional lightning lit flares that showed him glimpses of a weird nightmare of glistening rock and tumbling white water that caught the flame and hurled it in millions of tiny shafts on down the canyon.

The gray walked steadily, facing the wind but with bowed head, hesitating only occasionally to feel its way around some great rock or sudden, unexpected heap of debris.

The hoarse wind howled down the channel of rock, turning its shouting to a weird scream on corners where the pines feathered down into the passage of the wind. Battered by rain and wind, Rock Bannon bent his head and rode on, beaten, soaked, bedraggled, with no eyes to see, only trusting to the surefooted mountain horse and its blind instinct.

Once, when the lightning lifted the whole scene into stark relief, he glimpsed a sight that would never leave him if he lived to be a hundred. For one brief, all encompassing moment he saw the canyon as he never wanted to see it again.

The stallion had reached a bend, and, for a moment,

hesitated to relax straining, careful muscles. In that instant, the lightning flared.

Before them the canyon dropped steeply away like the walls of a gigantic stairway, black, glistening walls slanted by the steel of driving rain, cut by volleys of hail, and accompanied by the roar of the cataract below.

Two hundred feet down the white water roared, and banked in a cul-de-sac in the rock was a piled-up mass of foam, fifteen or twenty feet high, bulging and glistening. At each instant wind or water ripped some of it away and shot it, churning, down the fury of raging water below. Thunder roared a salvo, and the echoes responded, and the wild cliff clinging cedar threshed madly in the wind as if to tear free its roots and blow away to some place of relief from the storm.

Lightning crackled, and thunder drummed against the cliffs, and the scene blacked out suddenly into abysmal darkness. The steel-dust moved on, rounding the point of the rock, and starting to climb. Then, as if by a miracle, they were out of the canyon, but turning up a narrow crevice in the rock with water rushing, inches deep, beneath the stallion's feet. A misstep here and they would tumble down the crevice and pitch off into the awful blackness above the water. But the stallion was steady, and suddenly they came out on the swell of the mountain slope.

The lightning below was nothing compared to this. Here darkness was a series of fleeting intervals shot through with thunderbolts, and each jagged streak lighted the night like a blaze from Hades. Gaunt shoulders of the mountain butted against the bulging weight of cloud, and the skeleton fingers of long-dead pines felt stiffly of the wind.

Stunned by the storm, the stallion plodded on, and Rock swayed in the saddle, buffeted and hammered, as they walked across that bare, dead slope among the boulders, pushing relentlessly against the massive wall of the wind. A flash of lightning and a tree ahead detonated like a shell, and bits of it flew off into space with the wild complaint of a ricocheted bullet. The stub of the tree smoked, sputtered with flame, and went out, leaving a vague smell of charred wood and brimstone.

A long time later, dawn felt its way over the mountains beyond and behind him, and the darkness turned gray, and then rose as flame climbed the peaks. Rock rode on, sodden, beaten, overburdened with weariness. The high cliffs behind him turned their rust-colored heights to jagged bursts of frozen flame, but he did not notice. Weary, the stallion plodded down the last mile of slope and into the rain-flattened grass of the plain.

The valley was empty. Rock lifted his red-rimmed eyes and stared south. He saw no horsemen, no movement. He had beaten them. He would be home before they came. And once he was home and could stand beside the big old man who called him son, they would face their trouble together.

Let Harper come; he would learn what fighting meant. These men were not of the same flesh or the same blood, but the response within them was the same, and the fire that shaped the steel of their natures was the same. They were men bred to the Colt. Bred to the law of strength. Men who knew justice, but could fight to defend what was theirs, and what they believed.

He was not thinking that. He was thinking nothing. He was only moving, and the steel-dust walked on into the ranch yard. Rock fell rather than stepped from the saddle. Springer rushed out to get his horse.

"My stars, man! How'd you get here?"

"Over the mountain," Bannon said, and walked toward the house.

Awed, Springer turned and looked toward the towering, six-thousand-foot ridge. "Over the mountain," he said. "Over the mountain!" He stripped the saddle from the big horse and turned it into the corral, and then almost ran to the bunkhouse to tell Turner. "Over the mountain!"

Hardy Bishop looked up from his great chair and his eyes sharpened. Rock raised a hand, then walked on through the room, stripping off his soaked clothing as he went. When he reached the bed he pulled off one boot, then rolled over and stretched out, his left spur digging into the blanket.

Bishop followed him to the room and stared down at him grimly; then he walked back and dropped into the chair. Well, he reflected, for that he could be thankful. He had a man for a son. . . .

It had been a long time ago when he first came into this valley with old John Day. They had come down through the Narrows and looked out over the wide, beautiful length of it, and he had seen what he knew he was looking for—he had seen Paradise.

There were men in the West then, men who roamed the streams for beaver or the plains for buffalo. They lived and traded and fought with the Indians, learned their ways and went them one better. They pushed on into new country, country no white man had seen.

There were men like John Coulter, who first looked into the Yellowstone region, old Jim Bridger who knew the West as few men did. There were John Day, Smith, Hoback, Wilbur Price Hunt, Kit Carson and Robert Stuart. Most of them came for gold, but there were a few even then who looked for homes, and of the first was Hardy Bishop.

He had settled here, buying the land from the Indians, and trading with them long before any other white man remained in the region. Once a whole year had passed during which he saw not even one trapper.

The Kaws were usually his friends, but the Crows were not, and occasionally raiding parties of Blackfeet came down from the north. When they were friendly, he talked or traded, and when they wanted to fight, he fought.

After a while even the Crows left him alone, learning friendship was more profitable than death, and many had died. . . .

Bad days were coming. From his seat in the hidebound chair, Hardy Bishop could see that. The trouble with Indians would be nothing to the trouble with white men, and he was glad that Rock was a man who put peace first, but who handled a fast gun.

He raised his great head, his eyes twinkling. They were keen eyes that could see far and well. Even the Indians respected them. He could, they said, trail a snake across a flat rock, or a duck downstream through rough water. What he saw now was a horseman, riding toward the ranch. One lone horseman, and there was something odd in the way he rode.

It was not a man. It was a woman—a white woman. Hardy Bishop heaved himself ponderously from the chair. It had been almost ten years since he had seen a white woman! He walked slowly to the door, hitching his guns around, just in case.

The sun caught her hair and turned it to living flame. His dark eyes kindled. She rode up to the steps, and he saw Springer and Turner in the bunkhouse door, gaping. She swung down from her black mare and walked over to him. She was wearing trousers and a man's shirt. Her throat was bare in the open neck. He smiled. Here was a woman!

Sharon looked up at Bishop, astonished. Somehow, she had always known he would be big, but not such a monster of a man. Six-four he stood in his socks, and he weighed three hundred pounds. His head was covered with a shock of iron-gray hair, in tight curls. His eyes twinkled, and massive forearms and hands jutted from his sleeves.

"Come in! Come in!" he boomed. "You'll be Sharon Crockett, then. I've heard of you. Heard a sight of you!" He looked around as she hesitated on the steps. "What's the matter? Not afraid of an old man, are you? Come in."

"It isn't that. Only we've come here like this—and it was your land, and—"

"Don't explain." He shook his head. "Come in and sit down. You're the first white woman who ever walked into this house. First one ever saw it, I reckon. Rock, he's asleep. Dead to the world."

"He's safe then?" she asked. "I was afraid. I saw them go after him."

"There was trouble?" he looked at her keenly. "What happened?"

She explained the killing of Pete Zapata, and what happened afterward. "That's why I'm here," she said. "In a way, I'm asking for peace. We didn't know. We were foolish not to have listened to Rock in the beginning, when he told us about Mort. My father and the settlers want peace. I don't know about Pike Purcell and Lamport, but I can speak for the rest of us."

Bishop nodded his head. "Rock told me what he was goin' for. So he killed Zapata? That'll please the boys." He turned his head. "Dave!" he bellowed.

A face covered with a shock of mussed hair and beard shoved into the door. "Bring us some coffee! And some of that cake! We've got a lady here, by—" He flushed. "Excuse me, ma'am. Reckon my manners need a goin' over. We cuss a sight around here. A sight too much, I reckon. I ain't never figured on gettin' into heaven, anyways. I been pretty much of a sinner, and not much of a repenter. Reckon they'd have to widen the gate some, anyway; I'd be a sight of weight to get in. Most likely they'd have to put some cribbin' under the cloud I set on, too."

He chuckled, looking at her. "So you're the girl what's goin' to marry Rock?"

She jumped, and flushed. "Why! Why, I—"

"Don't let it get you down, ma'am! Reckon I'm a blunt old codger. It's true enough, the boy ain't said a word to me about it, but I can see what's in his eyes. I ain't raised the lad for nothin'. When he took off on this rampage, I was hopin' he'd find himself a gal. You like him, ma'am?" He looked at her sharply, his eyes filled with humor. "You goin' to marry him?"

"Why, I don't know," she protested. "I don't know that he wants me."

"Now listen here! Don't you go givin' me any of that demure, folded-hands palaver. That may go for those young bucks, but not for me. You know's well as I do if a woman sets her cap for a man he ain't got a chance. Only if he runs. That's all! Either give up and marry the gal or get clean out of the country and don't leave no address behind. Nor no trail sign, either!

"You might fool some young sprout with that he-hasn't-asked-me business, but not me. I seen many a young buck Indian give twenty head of ponies for some squaw when he could have had better ones for ten. Just because she wanted him like, and caused him to figure the price was cheap. No, sir! I'd rather try to get away from a bear trap on each foot and each hand, than a woman with her head set on marriage."

Flushed with embarrassment, she ignored what he had said. "Then—then, you'll let us have peace, sir? You won't be fighting us if we draw off from Harper?"

"Of course not, ma'am! I reckon it'd be a right nice thing to have a few folks around once in a while!" His eyes flashed. "But no more, you understand. Only this bunch of yours. No more!"

"And we can have our land, then?" she persisted.

"Sure, you can have it. You can have what them other fellows got, too, when they get out. Sure, you can have it. I can't set my hand to paper on it, though, because I never did learn to write. That's true, ma'am! Never learned to write, nor to read. But I can put my name on the side of a house with a six-shooter. I can do that. But them pens! They always figured to be a sight too small

for my hands. No, I can't read printin', but I can read
sign. I trailed a Blackfoot that stole a horse from me clean
to Montany one time. Trailed him six hundred miles,
believe me or not. Yes, ma'am, I come back with the
horse and an Indian scalp. Took it right in his own
village."

A startled yell rang out and Springer burst through the
door.

"Boss! Boss! Here they come! Oh, quick, man! Here
they—"

His voice died in the report of a gun, and Hardy Bishop
lunged from his chair to see men charging the porch.

Turner had started from the bunkhouse, but the rush
of the horses rode him down and they heard his wild,
agonized screams as he went down under the pounding
hoofs. Sharon never saw the old man reach for his guns,
but suddenly they were spouting flame and she saw a
man stagger back from the door, clutching at his breast
blood pouring over his hand.

Then a wild figure wearing one boot, appeared from
the other room swinging gunbelts about his hips. Then
Rock Bannon, too, was firing.

A sound came at the rear window, and Rock turned and
fired from the hip and the dark form looming there vanished. The attack broke, and Rock Bannon rushed to the
rifle rack and jerked down a Henry rifle. Then he grabbed
another and ran back, thrusting one at Bishop.

The old man dropped to his knees beside a window.
"Come up on us fast!" he said. "I was talkin' to this gal."

Rock's eyes swung to her, and then amazement faded
to sudden grimness. With horrer, she saw suspicion mount
in his eyes.

A wild chorus of yells sounded from outside, and then
a volley of shots smashed through the windows. The lamp
scattered in a thousand pieces, and from the kitchen they
heard cursing, then the crash of a buffalo gun.

"How many did you see?" Rock demanded.

"Most like a dozen," Bishop said. "We got two or three that first rush!"

"A dozen?" He wheeled to the girl. "Did the settlers come? Did they? Are they fighting us now?"

"Can't be that," Bishop said, staring out at the ranch yard, his eyes probing the corral. "No chance of that. This girl come with peace talk."

"And while she was talking, they rode in on us!" Rock raged.

Sharon came up, her eyes wide. "Oh, you can't believe that. You can't! I—"

The thud of bullets into the logs of the house drowned her voice, and the crashing of guns. Rock Bannon was slipping from window to window, moving on his feet like an Indian. He had yanked off his other boot now. A shot smashed the water olla that hung near the door. Bannon fired, and a man toppled from behind the corner of the corral and sprawled on the hard-packed ground near the body of Turner.

"They're goin' to rush us," Bannon said suddenly. He began loading his Colts. "Get set, Hardy. They're goin' to rush."

"Let 'em come! The sneak-thievin', pelt-robbin', trap-lootin' scum! Let 'em come! More'll come than'll go back!"

As the outlaws rushed suddenly, charging in a scattered line, the old man burst through the door, his Colt smoking.

A man screamed and grabbed his middle, took three staggering steps, and then sprawled his full length on the ground. Another man went down, and then a gun bellowed and the old man winced, took another step and then toppled back into the room.

Sharon stared at him in horror, and then ran to him. He looked shocked.

"Hit me! They hit me! Give me my gun, ma'am. I'll kill the scum like the wolverines they are!"

"S-sh, be still," she whispered. She began tearing the shirt away from the massive chest to search for the bullet wound.

Steadily, using now one gun, then the other, Rock Bannon fired. He could sense uncertainty among the attackers. They had shot the old man, but four of their own number were down, and probably others wounded. They were beginning to lose all desire for battle.

Watching closely, Rock saw a flicker of movement behind a corral trough. He watched, lifted his rifle, took careful aim, and when the movement came again, he fired, just under the trough.

A yell rang out and he saw a man lift up to his full height, then topple over.

"All right!" Bannon shouted. "Come on and get me! You wanted me! But you'd better come before the boys get in from north camp or they'll spoil my fun."

They wouldn't believe him, but it might make them doubtful. He heard voices raised in argument. Then there was silence. He reloaded all the guns, his own, Bishop's Henry, and the old man's six-guns. It was mid-afternoon, and the sun was hot. If they waited until night, he was going to have a bad time of it.

There was a chance, however, that they would believe his story, or fear that someone from the line cabin might ride far enough this way to hear the shots. If both groups came, they would be caught between two fires and wiped out.

An hour passed, and there was no sound.

"Rock!" Sharon was standing behind him. "We'd better get him on a bed."

He avoided her eyes, but got up and put his rifle down. It was a struggle, but they lifted Bishop off the floor and put him on his homemade four-poster. While Sharon bent over him, bathing the wound and treating it as best she could, Rock walked back to the windows.

Like a caged panther, he prowled from window to window. Outside all was still. Only the bodies of the dead lay on the hard-packed ground of the ranch yard. A dust devil started somewhere on the plain and twisted in the grass of the meadow, then skipped across the ranch yard, stirring around the body of Turner, and blowing in his hair.

Turner was dead. The old man had been with them almost as long as Rock himself. He had been like one of the family. And Bob Springer was gone, blasted from life suddenly, taking away all the young man's enthusiastic plans for a ranch of his own. Well, they would pay. They would pay to the last man.

The steel-dust stallion had come back from the end of the corral near the creek. He seemed curious and approached the body lying near the trough with delicate feet, ready to shy. He snuffed at the body, caught the scent of blood and jerked away, eyes distended and nostrils wide.

There was no one in sight; apparently the attackers had drawn off. They had anticipated no such defense as this. They had no idea that Rock Bannon was home, nor did they realize what a fighter the old man could be. They had to learn what the Crows had learned, long since.

Rock waited another hour, continuing his slow prowl. Within the house he was comparatively safe, and he knew that to go out before he was sure was to tempt fate. From time to time he went into the bedroom where Bishop lay on the four-poster. He was unconscious or asleep, Sharon sitting beside him.

He avoided her eyes, yet the thought kept returning, filling him with bitterness, that she had ridden here with peace talk, and under cover of her talk Harper's men had made their approach. Knowing Bishop, he knew that unless his attention had been diverted, no rider or group of riders could have reached the ranch without being seen.

Had she planned that with Mort Harper? Everything he knew about the girl compelled him to believe she would do nothing of the kind, yet the thought persisted, and it was almost too much of a coincidence.

After all, what reason had he to believe otherwise? Hadn't she admired Harper? Hadn't Pete Zapata been waiting in her cabin for him? Perhaps she had tried to warn him by throwing sticks on the fire, or it could have been an accident. The fact remained that in visiting her he had been almost killed in a trap laid by Zapata, and while she was making peace talk with Bishop, the raiding party had struck. It was not her fault they were not dead, both of them.

He knew she came to the door from time to time, and once she started to speak, then turned away as he avoided her eyes.

Rock was crouching by a window when the sound of horse's hoofs brought him to his feet. It was Bat Chavez, astride a slim, fast buckskin. The horse shied violently at Turner's body, and Bat had a hard time getting him to the door.

Bannon rushed out. "Everything all right at the line cabin?"

"Shucks, man!" Bat exploded. "That's what I was goin' to ask you. What happened here?"

"They hit us. Dave opened up from the kitchen, Hardy and I shot it out up here. Bishop's down, hit pretty bad. They got Springer and Turner, as you can see."

"Saw them cuttin' across the valley for Poplar a few minutes ago. The boys are gettin' restless, Rock. They want to ride over and wind this up."

"No more than I do," Bannon said shortly. "Yes, we're goin'. We'll ride over and wipe that place out."

"Oh, no! You mustn't!" Sharon had come to the door behind Rock. "Please, Rock! You musn't. The settlers don't want to fight any more. It's just Harper's crowd."

"Maybe that's true," Bannon said, "but I've seen no sign of them quittin' yet. There were at least twelve men in this bunch. Did Harper have twelve men of his own? Not that I saw, he didn't. And Zapata's dead. So's Miller. Where would he get twelve men?"

He turned back to Chavez. "Get some food into you, Bat, then ride back. I'll be down before long, and when I do, we'll cross that valley. If the settlers get in the way, they'll get what the rest of them got—what they gave Turner and Springer here! We've dallied long enough." Rock Bannon turned and walked back into the house.

Sharon stared at him, her face white. "Then you won't believe me?" she protested. "You'll go over there and kill innocent people?"

"Who killed Springer and Turner?" Rock demanded sharply. "In what way had they offended? I don't know that your settlers are innocent. I tried to tell them what they were going into and they wouldn't believe me. Well, they came, and if they get their tails in a crack they've only themselves to blame.

"I argued with them. I argued with Bishop to give them a break, and now this happens. There were twelve men in that attack on us. At least twelve! Well, some of them died out here, but you and I both know that Harper didn't have twelve men. Perhaps eight, at best. They came in here and killed two of our boys and wounded Bishop. That old man in there has been a father to me. He's been more than most fathers. He's been a guide and a teacher, and all I know I learned from him. He may die. If he does the fault was mine for ever letting this bunch of squatters in here."

The girl clasped her hands in distress. "Please, Rock," she protested, "you can't do this. Most of your men don't know one from the other. The settlers would be killed whether they fought or not. Their homes will be burned."

"If they don't fight they won't be hurt," he insisted stubbornly. "Next time that Harper attacks, he might get us all. Anyway, it looks to me as if they were plenty willing to ride in on Harper's coattails and get all they could while the getting was easy."

"That's not true," she protested hotly. "They wanted to do the right thing. They thought they were doing the right thing. They believed Harper was honest."

Rock slid into his buckskin coat and picked up his hat. His face was grim and hard. He could not look at Sharon, and knew if their eyes met it would tear the heart out of him. Yet he knew he had waited too long now, that if he had resorted to guns long ago so many things might not have happened. Springer might be living, and Turner, and Collins, the settler.

He started for the door, picking up his rifle from where he had left it. "Rock," Sharon said, "if you go back, I will, too. The first one of your men who puts a hand on a settler's home, I'll kill with my own rifle."

For the first time he looked at her, and her eyes were flashing with pain and anger. "Go then!" he said brutally. "But if you're half as smart as I think you are, you'll take your friends and head for the hills. Go! I'll give you a start. Warn Harper, too, if you want. Let him know we're coming. But if you want to save that precious pack of settlers, get them out of Poplar. Take to the hills until this is over—but be out of town before my boys ride in!"

He walked to the door and went out. She saw him stop by the corral and pick up a rope, then go to the corral for the steel-dust. Running from the house, she threw herself into the saddle of her own black mare, tied at the corner of the house, and spurring to top speed, sprang out on the long ride across the valley.

Rock Bannon did not look up, nor turn his head, but

in his heart and mind the hard hoofs pounded like the pulse in his veins, pounded harder and harder, then vanished with the dying sound of the running horse.

He saddled the gray, and as Bat Chavez walked from the house, Rock swung into the saddle. "Dave!" he yelled at the cook. "You watch over Hardy. We won't be gone long."

Abruptly, he swung the stallion south. Chavez rode beside him, glancing from time to time at Rock. Finally, he burst out. "Bannon, I think that gal's on the level. I sure do!"

"Yes?" Rock did not turn his head. "You let me worry about that!"

VIII

PIKE PURCELL was a grim and lonely man. He had been loitering all day around the saloon. Only that morning, before riding away to the attack on the Bishop ranch house in which he and Lamport had taken part, Dud Kitchen had told him about the bullet that killed Collins.

Pike was disturbed. His heart had not been in the fight at the ranch, and he had fired few shots. In fact, he and Lamport had been among the first to turn away from the fight. Purcell was thoroughly disillusioned in Mort Harper. The attack on the ranch had been poorly conceived and even more poorly carried out. Purcell didn't fancy himself as a leader, but he knew he could have done better.

Men had died back there—too many of them. Pike Purcell had a one-track mind and that one track was busy with surmises over the story told him by Dud. He could verify the truth of the supposition. Mort Harper had been behind Collins. It worried him, and his loyalty, already shaken by inadequate leadership, found itself on uncertain ground.

On the ride back, there had been little talk. The party was sullen and angry. Their attack had failed under the straight shooting of Bishop and Bannon. They were leaving six men behind, six men who were stone dead. Maybe they had killed two, but that didn't compensate for six. Bishop was down, but how badly none of them knew.

Cap Mulholland had ridden in the attack as well. Never strongly inclined toward fighting, he had no heart in this fight. He had even less now. Suddenly he was realizing with bitterness that he didn't care if he ever saw Mort Harper again.

"They'll be comin' for us now," Cap said.

"Shut up!" Lamport snapped. He was angry and filled with bitterness. He was the only one of the settlers who

101

had thrown in completely with Harper's crowd, and the foolishness of it was now apparent. Defeat and their own doubts were carrying on the rapid disintegration of the Harper forces. "You see what I saw?" he demanded. "That Crockett girl was there. She was the one dragged Bishop's body back. I seen her!"

Harper's head jerked up. "You lie!" he snapped viciously.

Lamport looked across at Harper. "Mort," he said evenly, "don't you tell me I lie."

Harper shrugged. "All right, maybe she was there, but I've got to see it to believe it. How could she have beaten us to it?"

"How did Bannon beat us back?" Lamport demanded furiously. "He was supposed to be lost in the hills."

"He must have come back over the mountain," Gettes put in. He was one of the original Harper crowd. "He must have found a way through."

"Bosh!" Harper spat. "Nothing human could have crossed that mountain last night. A man would be insane to try it."

"Well," Pike said grimly, "Bannon got there. I know good and well he never rode none of those canyons last night, so he must've come over the mountain. If any man could, he could."

Harper's eyes were hard. "You seem to think a lot of him," he sneered.

"I hate him," Pike snapped harshly. "I hate every step he takes, but he's all man!"

Mort Harper's face was cruel as he stared at Pike. Purcell had ridden on, unnoticing.

Pike did not return to his cabin after they reached Poplar. Pike Purcell was as just as he was ignorant and opinionated. His one quality was loyalty—that and more than his share of courage. Dud Kitchen's story kept cropping up. Did Harper own a small gun?

Suddenly, he remembered. Shortly after they arrived

at Poplar he had seen such a gun. It was a .34 Patterson, and Mort Harper had left it lying on his bed.

Harper was gone somewhere. The saloon was empty. Purcell stepped in, glanced around, then walked back to Harper's quarters. The room was neat, and things were carefully arranged. He glanced around, crossed to a rough wooden box on the far side of the room, and lifted the lid. There were several boxes of .44's, and a smaller box. Opening it, he saw a series of neat rows of .34-caliber cartridges, and across the lead nose of each shell was a deep notch!

He picked up one of the shells and stepped back. His face was gray as he turned toward the door. He was just stepping through when Mort Harper came into the saloon.

Quick suspicion came into Mort's eyes. "What are you doin' in there?" he demanded.

"Huntin' for polecat tracks," Purcell said viciously. "I found 'em!" He took the shell out and tossed it on the table. It was the wrong move, for it left his right hand outstretched and far from his gun.

At such a time things happen instantaneously. Mort Harper's hand flashed for his gun, and Purcell was far too late. He got his hand on the butt when the bullet struck him. He staggered back, hate blazing in his eyes, and sat down hard. He tugged at his gun, and Harper shot him again.

Staring down at the body of the tall old mountaineer, Mort Harper saw the end of everything. So this was how things finished? An end to dreams, an end to ambition. He would never own the greatest cattle empire in the West, a place where he would be a king on his own range with nothing to control his actions but his own will.

He had despised Purcell for his foolishness in following him. He had led the settlers like sheep, but now they would survive and he would die. In a matter of hours, even minutes, perhaps, Bannon would be here, and then nothing would be left but a ruin.

At that moment he heard a pounding of horse's hoofs and looked up to see Sharon go flying past on her black mare.

There was something left. There was Sharon. Rock Bannon wanted her. Sudden resolution flooded him. She was one thing Bannon wouldn't get! Mort Harper ran to his quarters and threw a few things together, then walked out. Hastily, under cover of the pole barn, he saddled a fresh horse, loaded his gear aboard, and swung into the saddle and started up the canyon toward the Crockett home.

Cap Mulholland watched him go, unaware of what was happening. Dud Kitchen had heard the shots, and had returned for his own guns. He watched Harper stop at the Crockett place, unaware of the stuffed saddlebags. When he saw the man swing down, he was not surprised.

Sharon had caught Jim Satterfield in the open and told him they should flee the village at once. At this moment Satterfield was headed for the Pagones house as fast as he could move. Sharon ran into the house, looking for her father, but he was in the fields. There was not a moment to lose. She ran out, and was just swinging into the saddle when Mort Harper dismounted at the front steps. He heard her speak to the horse, and stepped around the house.

"Sharon!" he said. "You're just in time."

She halted. "What do you mean?" she demanded coolly.

He rushed to her excitedly. "We're leaving! We must get away now. Just you and me! The Bishop crowd will be coming soon, and they'll leave nothing here. We still have time to get away."

"I'm going to get my father now," she said. "Then we'll go to the hills."

"There's no time for that—he'll get along. You come with me!" Harper was excited, and he did not see the danger lights in Sharon's eyes.

"Go where?" she inquired.

Mort Harper stared at her impatiently. "Away! Anywhere, for the time being. Later we can go on to California together, and—"

"Aren't you taking too much for granted?" She reached for the black mare's bridle. "I'm not going with you, Mort. I'm not going anywhere with you."

It was a real shock. He stared at her, unbelieving and impatient. "Don't be foolish!" he snapped. "There's nothing for you here. You were practically promised to me. If it's marriage you want, don't worry about that. We can go on to California, and be married there."

"It is marriage I want, Mort, but not to you. Never to you. For a little while I was as bad as the others. I believed in you, and then I saw the kind of men you had around you, how you'd deliberately led us here to use us for your own ends. No, Mort. I'm not marrying you and I'm not going away with you." She made no attempt to veil the contempt in her voice. "If you're afraid, you'd better get started. I'm going for my father."

Suddenly he was calm, dangerously calm. "So? It's that Rock Bannon, is it? I never thought you'd take that ignorant cowhand seriously. Or," he sneered, "is it your way of getting Bishop's Valley?"

"Get out!" she said. "Get out now! Dad and Pagones will be here in a moment and when I tell them what you've said, they'll kill you."

"Kill me? Those two?" He laughed. Then his face stiffened. "All right, I'll get out, but you're coming with me!"

He moved so swiftly she had no chance to defend herself. He stepped toward her suddenly, and she saw his fist start. The shock of the blow was scarcely greater than the shock of the fact that he had struck her. Dimly, she realized he had thrown her into the saddle and was lashing her there. She thought she struggled, but she lived those moments only in a half-world of consciousness, a half-world soon pounded into oblivion by the drum of racing horses.

It was Satterfield who finally got Crockett from the fields. The Bishop riders were already in sight when Tom raced into his house, caught up his rifle, and called for Sharon. She was gone, and he noted that her black mare was gone. She was away, that was the main thing. With Jim, he ran out into the field where he was joined by Pagones, his wife, daughter and Dud Kitchen.

The others were coming. It was a flight, and there was no time to prepare or take anything but what lay at hand. Cap Mulholland, his face sullen, went with them, his wife beside him. The Olsens and Greenes joined them, and in a compact group they turned away toward the timber along the hillside.

Lamport did not go. He had no idea that Mort Harper was gone. John Kies was in his store, waiting the uncertain turn of events. Kies had worked with Mort before, and he trusted the younger man's skill and judgment.

It was over. It was finished. Lamport stared cynically at the long buildings of the town. Probably it was just as well, for he would do better in the gold fields. Steady day-to-day work had never appealed to him. Pike Purcell had been an honest but misguided man; Lamport was neither. From the first he had sensed the crooked grain in the timber of Mort Harper, but he didn't care.

Lamport felt that he was self-sufficient. He would stay in as long as the profits looked good, and he would get out when the luck turned against them. He had seen the brilliant conception of theft that had flowered in the brain of Mort Harper. He saw what owning that valley could mean.

It was over. He had lived and worked with Purcell, but he had no regret for the man. Long ago he had sensed that Harper would kill him some day. Of all the settlers, Lamport was the only one who had read Harper right, and perhaps because they were of the same feeling.

Yet there was a difference. Lamport's hate was a tangible, deadly thing. Harper could hate and he could fight, but Harper was completely involved with himself. He could plot, wait, and strike like a rattler. Lamport had courage with his hate, and that was why he was not running now. He was waiting, waiting in the full knowledge of what he faced.

His hate for Rock Bannon had begun when Bannon rode so much with Sharon. It had persisted, developing from something much deeper than any rivalry over a woman. It developed from the innate, basic rivalry of two strong men, two fighting men, each of whom recognizes in the other a worthy and dangerous foe.

Lamport had always understood Harper. Of all those that had surrounded him, Lamport was the only one Mort Harper had feared. Pete Zapata he had always believed he could kill. Lamport was the one man with whom he avoided trouble. He even avoided conversation with him when possible. He knew Lamport was dangerous, and he knew he would face him down if it came to that.

He was a big man, as tall as Rock Bannon, and twenty pounds heavier. When he walked his head thrust forward somewhat and he stared at the world from pale blue eyes beneath projecting shelves of beetling brows. In his great shoulders there was a massive, slumbering power. Lamport's strength had long since made him contemptuous of other men, and his natural skill with a gun had added to that contempt. He was a man as brutal as his heavy jaw, as fierce as the light in his pale eyes.

Surly and sullen, he made friends with no one. In the biting envy and cantankerousness of Pike Purcell he had found companionship, if no more. Lamport was not a loyal man. Purcell's death meant nothing to him. He waited for Rock Bannon, now filled with hatred for the victor in the fight, the man who would win.

Thinking back now, Lamport could see that Rock had always held the winning hand. He had known about

Bishop, was a kin to him, had known what awaited here. Also, from the start his assay of Harper's character had been correct.

From the beginning, Lamport had accepted the partnership with Purcell, rode with the wagon train because it was a way west, and threw in with Harper for profit. In it all, he respected but one man, the man he was now waiting to kill.

When, in the deserted bar, he heard the horses coming, he poured another drink. Somewhere, there were three or four more men. The rest had vanished like snow in a desert sun. Hitching his guns into place, he walked to the door and out on the plank porch.

John Kies's white face stared at him from an open window of the store.

"Where's Mort?" Kies asked. "That's them coming now."

Lamport chuckled and spat into the dust. He scratched the stubble on his heavy jaw and grinned sardonically at Kies.

"He's around, I reckon, or maybe he blowed out. The rest of 'em have."

Stark fear came into the storekeeper's face. "No! No, they can't have!" he protested. "They'll have an ambush! they'll—"

"You're crazy!" Lamport sneered. "This show is busted. You know that. That's Bannon comin' now, and when that crowd of his gets through, there won't be one stick on another in this town."

"But the settlers!" Kies wailed. "They'll stop him."

Lamport grinned at him. "The settlers have took to the hills. They're gone! Me, I'm waitin' to kill Rock Bannon. Then if I can fight off his boys, I'm goin'."

They came up the street, walking their horses. Rock was in the lead, his rifle across his saddle bows. To his right was Bat Chavez, battle-hungry as always. To his left was Red, riding loosely on a paint pony. Behind them, in a mounted skirmishing line, came a dozen hard-bitten Indian-fighting plainsmen, riders for the first big cow spread north of Texas.

A rifle shot rang out suddenly from a cabin in back of the store. Then another. A horse staggered and went down, and Bat Chavez wheeled his horse, and with four riders, raced toward the cabin. The man who waited there lost his head suddenly and bolted.

A lean blond rider in a Mexican jacket swept down on him, rope twirling. It shot out, and the horse went racing by, and the burly teamster's body was a bounding thing, leaping and tumbling through the cactus after the racing horse. Chavez swung at once, and turned back toward the saloon. The riders fanned out and started going through the town. Where they went, there were gunshots, then smoke.

Rock Bannon saw Lamport standing on the porch. "Don't shoot!" he commanded. He walked the steel-dust within twenty feet. Lamport stood on the edge of the porch, wearing two guns, his dark, dirty red wool shirt open at the neck to display a massive, hairy chest.

"Howdy, Rock!" Lamport said. He spat into the dust. "Come to take your lickin'?"

"To give you yours," Rock said coolly. "How do you want it?"

"Why, I reckon we're both gun-handy, Rock," Lamport said, "so I expect it'll be guns. I'd have preferred hand-fightin' you, but that would scarcely give you an even break."

"You reckon not?" Rock slid from the stallion. "Well, Lamport, I always figure to give a man what he wants. If you think you can take me with your hands, shed those guns and get started. You've bought yourself a fight."

Incredulous, Lamport stared at him. "You mean it?" he said, his eyes brightening.

"Stack your duds and grease your skids, coyote!" Rock said. "It's knuckle and skull now, and free fighting, if you like it!"

"Free, he says!" A light of unholy joy gleamed in Lamport's eyes. "Free it is!"

"Watch yourself, boss!" Red said, low-voiced. "That hombre looks like blazin' brimstone on wheels!"

"Then we'll take off his wheels and kick the brimstone out!" Rock said. He hung his guns over the saddlehorn as Bat Chavez rode around the corner.

Lamport faced him in the dust before the saloon, a huge, grizzly of a man with big iron knuckled hands and a skin that looked like a stretched rawhide.

"Come and get it!" he sneered, and rushed.

As he rushed, he swung a powerful right. Rock Bannon met him halfway, and lashed out with his own right. His punch was faster, and it caught the big man flush, but Lamport took it on the mouth, spat blood, and rushed in swinging with both fists. Suddenly he caught Bannon and hurled him into the dust with such a force that a cloud of dust arose. Rock rolled over like a cat, gasping for breath, and just rolled from under Lamport's driving boots as the big man tried to leap on him to stamp his life out.

Rock scrambled to his feet, and lunged as he picked his hands out of the dust, butting Lamport in the chest. The big renegade jerked up a stiff thumb, trying for Rock's eye, but Bannon rolled his head away and swung a left to the wind, and then a driving right that ripped Lamport's ear, starting a shower of blood.

Lamport now charged again and caught Bannon with two long swings on the head. His skull roaring with pain and dizziness, Rock braced himself and started to swing in a blind fury, both hands going with every ounce of power he could muster.

Lamport met him and, spraddle-legged, the two started to slug. Lamport was the bigger, and his punches packed terrific power, but were a trifle slower. It was nip and tuck, dog eat dog, and the two battled until the breath gasped in their lungs and whistled through their teeth. Lamport ducked his battered face and started to walk in, stemming the tide of Bannon's blows by sheer physical power.

Rock shifted his attack with lightning speed. He missed a right, and following it in with the weight of his body, slid his arm around Lamport's thick neck, grabbed the wrist with his left hand, and jerked up his feet and sat down hard, trying to break Lamport's neck.

But the big renegade knew all the tricks, and as Rock's feet flew up, Lamport hurled his weight forward and to the left, falling with his body half across Bannon. It broke the hold, and they rolled free. Rock came to his feet, and Lamport, catlike in his speed, lashed out with a wicked kick for his head.

Rock rolled away from it and hurled himself at Lamport's one standing leg in a flying tackle. The big man went down, and as they scrambled up, Rock hit him with a left and right, splitting his right cheek in a bone-deep gash, and pulping his lips.

Lamport was bloody and battered now, yet he kept coming, his breath wheezing. Rock Bannon stabbed a left into his face, set himself and whipped up a right uppercut to the body. Lamport gasped. Bannon circled, then smashed him in the body with another right, then another and another. Lamport's jaw was hanging open now, his face battered and bleeding from a dozen cuts and abrasions. Rock walked in, measured him, then crossed a right to his chin. He followed it up with two thudding, bone-crushing blows, and Lamport reeled, tried to steady himself, and then measured his length in the dust.

Rock Bannon weaved on his feet, then walked to the watering trough and ducked his head into it. He came up spluttering, then splashed water over his face and body, stripping away the remnants of his torn shirt.

"We got 'em all, boss," Red said. "You want we should go after the settlers?"

"No, and leave their homes alone. Where's Kies?"

"The storekeeper? Inside, I guess."

Rock strapped 'on his guns and strode up the steps of the store with Red and Chavez at his heeels. Kies was waiting behind the counter, his face white.

"Kies," Rock said, "have you got the bills for the goods you sold the settlers?"

"The bills?" Kies's frightened eyes showed doubt, then dismay. "Why, yes."

"Get 'em out."

Fumblingly, Keis dug out the bills. Quickly, Bannon scanned through them. Then he took out a match and set fire to the stack as they lay on the counter.

Kies sprang for them. "What are you doing?"

"You're payin' the price of hookin' up with a crooked bunch," Bannon said grimly, as Chavez held the angry storekeeper. "You got a horse?"

"Yes, I have a—horse. But I—"

"Red," Bannon turned. "Give this man some shells, a rifle, a canteen and two days' grub—skimpy rations. Then put him on a horse and start him on his way. If he tries to load that rifle or if he doesn't ride right out of the country, hang him."

"But the Indians!" Keis protested. "And my store!"

"You haven't got a store," Bannon told him harshly. "You'll have to look out for the Indians yourself."

"Boss," Chavez touched him on the shoulder. "Hombres here want to talk."

Rock Bannon wheeled. Tom Crockett, Pagones and Dud Kitchen were standing there.

"Bannon," Crockett said, "Harper took my girl. Kitchen saw him tying her to a horse."

Rock's face went white, then stiffened. "I reckon he was the one she wanted," he said. "She had Zapata waitin' for me, and she led that raid to the ranch."

"No, she didn't do that, Rock," Pagones said. "The raid wasn't even organized when she left. As for Zapata—"

"He forced himself on us," Crockett protested. "And she was tied to the saddle. She didn't want to go with Harper. She loves you."

"That's right, Rock," Pagones assured him. "Mary's known that for weeks."

"All right," Rock said. He jerked a shirt from a stack on the counter and began getting into it. "I'll find 'em."

"Who goes along with you?" Bat asked eagerly.

"Nobody," Bannon said. "This is my job."

IX

T HE STEEL-DUST STALLION liked the feel of the trail. He always knew when he was going some place that was beyond the place where distance lost itself against the horizon. He knew it now, knew in the sound of Rock Bannon's voice and the easy way he sat in the saddle.

Rock rode through the poplars where the wagon train had spent its last night on the trail, and as he passed, he glanced down at the ruts, already grown with grass. It seemed such a long time ago, yet it was scarcely more than days since the wagons had waited here. He had observed them from the mountains, looking back for the last time as he rode away from the train.

He turned the stallion up the long, grassy canyon where Freeman had been killed. The trail Mort Harper had left was plain enough. So far he had been running, later he would try to cover it, yet already Bannon was looking ahead, planning, trying to foresee what plan, if any, could be in the man's mind.

The Day's River region was one of the most rugged in all America. No man knew it well, few knew it even passingly well. Unless a man chose carefully of the trails that it offered, he would run into a blind canyon, a trail that ended in a jump-off, or some blind tangle of boulders.

There were trails through; the Indians had used them. Other Indians, ages before, had left picture-writing on the canyon walls, some of them in places almost impossible to reach. No man living knew the history of this region.

There were places here with a history stranger than any written—an old weapon washed from the sands of a creek, a strange date on a canyon wall. There was one place miles from here where the date "1642" was carved on a canyon wall among other dates and names, and no man has yet accounted for that date, nor said who put it there, nor how he came to be in the country.

From Grass Canyon the trail of the two horses led into a narrow draw with very steep sides overgrown with birch, balsam and cottonwood. His rifle ready, although anticipating no trouble at this stage, Rock pushed on.

The draw now opened on a vast region of jagged mountain ridges, gorges, cliffs and mesas. The stallion followed the trail along the edge of a meadow watered by a brawling mountain stream. Some teal flew from the pool of water backed up by a beaver dam, and Rock heard the sharp, warning slap of the beaver's tail on the water.

The trail dipped now down a narrow passage between great rock formations that towered heavenward. On one side was an enormous mass of rock like veined marble, and on the other a rock of brightest orange fading to rust red, shot through with streaks of purple.

Boulders scattered the space between the walls, and at times passage became difficult. At one place great slabs of granite had sloughed off from high above and come crashing down upon the rocks below. Far ahead he could see the trail leaving the lowlands and climbing, thread-like, across the precipitous wall of the mountain.

Studying the trail and the speed of the horses he was following, Rock could see that Mort was trying for distance, and fast. Rock knew, too, that unless Harper was far ahead, he would, if watching his backtrail, soon know he was followed. From the incredible heights ahead the whole series of canyons and gorges would be plainly visible except when shoulders of rock or boulders intervened.

The trail up the face of the cliff had been hewn by nature from the solid rock itself, cutting across the face of an almost vertical cliff, and only emerging at times in bare rock ledges or dipping around some corner of rock into a cool, shadowed gorge.

"He's headin' for Big Track," Rock told himself suddenly. "He sure is. He's headin' for Big Track Hollow."

He knew the place, and certainly if Harper were following a known or planned route, he could choose no better. Big Track Hollow was a basin over six thousand feet above sea level where there was a wealth of grass, and plenty of water and sheltering woods.

This would be the best place in this region to hole up for any length of time. Long ago, somebody had built a cabin there, and there were caves in the basin walls. It took its name from gigantic dinosaur tracks that appeared in the rock all along one side.

For Harper the place had the distinct advantage of offering four separate avenues of escape; each would take him over a trail widely divergent from the others, so once a follower was committed to one trail he would have to retrace his steps and start over again to find his quarry. The time consumed would leave him so far behind that it would be impossible to catch up.

Rock Bannon stared thoughtfully at the tracks. It would soon be night, and the two must stop, yet they had sufficient lead on him to make it difficult to overtake them soon, and at night he could easily get off the trail and lose himself in the spiderweb of canyons.

Reluctantly, he realized he must camp soon. The landscape everywhere now was rock, red rock cliffs towering against the sky, cathedral shaped buttes and lofty pinnacles. He rode down the steep trail, dipping into shadowy depths and riding along a canyon that echoed with the stallion's steps. It was like riding down a long hallway carved from solid rock, lonely and empty.

There was no sound but the walking of the horse and the creak of the saddle leather. Dwarfed by the lofty walls, he moved like a ghost in a vast, unreal world, yet he rode warily, for at any point Harper might elect to stop and waylay him.

Now the trail down the long avenue between the walls

began to rise, and suddenly he emerged upon a plateau that seemed to hang upon the rim of the world.

Far away and below him stretched miles upon miles of the same broken country, but there were trees and grass in the valleys below, and he turned the horse at right angles, then reined in. Here for a space was gravel and rock. He studied the ground carefully, then moved on.

The trail was difficult now, and in the fading light he was compelled to slip from saddle, rifle in hand, and walk along over the ground. The trail wound around and around, steadily dropping. Then ahead of him he saw a pool, and beside it a place where someone had lain to drink.

Sliding to the ground, he stripped the saddle from the stallion and tethered him on a grassy plot. Then he gathered dry sticks for a fire, which he made, keeping it very small, in the shadow of some boulders. When the fire was going he made coffee, then slipped back from the fire and carefully scouted the surrounding darkness.

Every step of the way was a danger. Mort Harper was on the run now, and he would fight like a cornered rat, where and when and how he could find the means.

Before daylight Rock rolled out, packed his gear and saddled the stallion. Yet when it was light enough to see, there was no trail. The water of the stream offered the best possibility, so he rode into it himself, scanning the narrow banks with attention.

Finally, after being considerably slowed down by the painstaking search, he found where they had left the stream. A short distance further, after seeing no marks, he found a bruised clump of grass where a horse had stepped and slipped.

He had gone no more than four miles when he found where they had camped. There had been two beds, one back in a corner of rocks away from the other, and cut off from the trail by it. Mort Harper was taking no chances. Yet when Rock looked around, he glimpsed something under a bush in the damp earth.

Kneeling, he put his head under the bush. Scratched in the earth with a stick were the words, *Be Careful*, and then, *Big Track*.

He had been right then. Harper was headed for Big Track. If that were so, they were a good day's ride from there. Bannon thought that over while climbing the next ridge. Then he made a sudden decision. From the ridge, he examined the terrain before him, then wheeled his horse. As he did so a shot rang out. Leaping from the horse to a cleft in the rock, he lifted his rifle and waited.

The country on the other side of the ridge was fairly open, but with clumps of brush and boulders. To ride down there after a rifleman—and Harper was an excellent shot—would be suicide. Only his wheeling of the stallion had saved his life at that moment.

Sliding back from the cleft, he retreated down the hillside to the gray. He swung into saddle, and keeping the ridge between him and the unseen marksman, he started riding east. He had made his decision, and he was going to gamble on it.

If he continued to follow, as he was following now, he would fall further and further behind, compelled to caution by Harper's rifle and the difficulty of following the trail. If Harper reached Big Track Hollow first, it would be simple for him to take a trail out of there, and then it would be up to Bannon to find which trail.

Rock Bannon had never heard of a cutoff to Big Track, but he knew where he was, and he knew where Big Track was. Ahead of him a draw opened and he raced the steel-dust into it and started along it, slowing the horse to a canter. Ahead of him and on the skyline, a sharp pinnacle pointed at the sky. That was his landmark.

The country grew rougher, but he shifted from draw to draw, cut across a flat, barren plateau of scattered rocks and rabbit grass, traversed a lava flow, black and ugly, to skirt a towering rust red cliff. A notch in the cliff ahead seemed to indicate a point of entry, so he guided the stallion among the boulders. A lizard darted from under the stallion's hoofs, and overhead a buzzard wheeled in wide, lonely circles.

The sun was blazing-hot now, and the rocks caught and multiplied the heat. He skirted the gray, dirty mud shore of a small alkaline lake, and rode into a narrow cleft in the mountain.

At one point it was so narrow that for thirty yards he had to pull one foot from the stirrup and drag the stirrup up into the saddle. Then the cleft opened into a spacious green valley, its sides lined with a thick growth of quaking aspen. There was water here, and he stopped to give the stallion a brief rest and to drink.

They had been moving at a rapid clip for the distance and the heat, yet the horse looked good. Again he checked his guns. It was nip and tuck now. If he made Big Track before they reached it, or by the same time, he must hurry. If he failed, then there was not one chance in a dozen that he would ever see Sharon again.

Now, every movement, every thought, every inflection of her voice returned to him, filling him with desperation. She was his, and had always been his—not only, he understood now, in his own heart, but in hers. He had always known what Mort Harper was. He should never have doubted the girl. It was amazing to him now that he had doubted her for even an instant.

So on he went, though the sun blazed down on the flaming rocks in a torment and the earth turned to hot brass beneath the stallion's feet. The mountains grew rougher. There was more and more lava, and then when it seemed it could get no worse, he rode out upon a glaring white alkali desert that lasted for eight miles at midday, stifling dust and blazing sun.

Rock Bannon seemed to have been going for hours now, yet it was only because of his early start. It was past one in the afternoon, and he had been riding, with but one break, since four in the morning.

On the far side of the desert there was a spring of water that tasted like rotten eggs—mineral water. He drank a little, rubbed the horse down with a handful of rabbit grass, and let him graze briefly. Then he mounted again and went on, climbing into the hills.

Big Track was nearer, somewhere not far from the great sky-stabbing pinnacle he had seen. Sweat streamed down his face and down his body under his shirt. He squinted his eyes against the sun and the smart of the sweat. He had to skirt a towering peak to get to the vicinity of Big Track.

He was riding now with all thought lost, only his goal in mind, and a burning, driving lust to come face to face with Mort Harper. Somewhere ahead he would be waiting; somewhere ahead they would meet.

The sun brought something like delirium, and he thought again of the long days of riding over the plains, of Sharon's low voice and her cool hands as he wrestled with pain and fever, recovering from the wounds of a lone battle against Indians. He seemed to feel again the rocking roll of the wagon over the rutted, dusty trail, tramped by the thousands heading for the new lands in the West.

Why had he waited so long to speak? Why hadn't he been able to find words to tell the girl he loved her? Words had always left him powerless; to act was easy, but somehow to shape the things he felt into words was beyond him, and women put so much emphasis on words, on the saying of things, and the way they were said.

He swung down from the saddle after a long time and walked on, knowing even the great stallion's strength was not without limit. The wild, strange country through which he was going now was covered with blasted boulders, the rough, slaglike lava, and scattered pines, dwarfish and wind-bedraggled, whipped into agonized shapes by the awful contortions of the wind.

Then he saw the stark pinnacle almost ahead, and he saw, beyond it, the green of the Big Track. He climbed back into the saddle again, and mopped the sweat from his face. The big horse walked wearily now, but the goal was reached. Rock Bannon loosened the guns in their holsters, and, grim-faced, he turned down a natural trail that no man had ridden before him, and into the green lush splendor of Big Track Hollow.

The smell of the grass was rich and almost unbelievable, and he heard a bird singing, and the sudden whir of wings as some game bird took off in sudden flight. Water sounded, and the gray stallion quickened his pace. He skirted a wide-boled aspen and rode through a grass scattered with purple and pink asters, white sego lilies, and red baneberry. Then he saw the water, and rode rapidly toward it.

He dropped from saddle, taking a quick look around. No human sound disturbed the calm, utter serenity of Big Track. He dropped to his chest on the ground and drank, and beside him, the steel-dust drank deep.

Suddenly, the stallion's head came up sharply. Warned, Rock felt his every muscle tense. Then, he forced himself to relax. The horse was looking at something, the calling of birds was stilled. He got slowly to his feet, striving to avoid any sudden movement, knowing in every muscle and fiber of his being that he was being watched. He turned, slowly, striving for a casual, careless manner.

Mort Harper was standing a short distance away, a pistol in his hand. He was thinner, wolfish now, his face darkened by sun and wind, his eyes hard and cruel. Backed in a corner, all the latent evil of the man had come to the fore. Quick fear touched Rock.

"Howdy," he said calmly. "I see you're not takin' any

chances, Mort. Got that gun right where it'll do the most good."

Harper smiled, and with his teeth bared he looked even more vulpine, even more cruel. "We both know what it means to get the drop," Harper said. "We both know it means you're a dead man."

"I ain't so sure," Bannon said, shrugging. "I've heard of men who beat it. Maybe I'm one of the lucky ones."

"You don't beat this one," Mort said grimly. "I'm going to kill you." Suddenly his eyes darkened with fury. "I'd like to know how in blazes you got here!" he snapped.

"Figured you'd head for this place if you knew the country at all," Bannon replied with a shrug. "So I cut across country."

"There's no other trail," Harper said. "It can't be done."

Rock Bannon stared at him coldly. "Where I want to go, there's always a trail," Bannon said. "I make my own trails, Mort Harper, I don't try to follow and steal the work of other men."

Harper laughed. "That doesn't bother me, Rock. I've still got the edge. Maybe I lost on that steal, but I've got your woman. I've got her, and I'll keep her! Oh, she's yours, all right—I know that now. She's yours, and a hellcat with it, but it'll be fun breaking her, and before I take her out of these hills she'll be broken—or dead.

"I've got her, and she's fixed so if anything happens to me, you'll never find her and she'll die there alone. It'll serve both of you right. Only I'm not going to die—you are."

"All rat," Rock said coldly. "A rat all the way through. I don't imagine you ever had a square, decent thought in your life. Always out to get something cheap, to beat somebody, to steal somebody else's work, and fancying yourself a smart boy because of it."

Rock Bannon smiled suddenly. "All right, you're going to kill me. Mind if I smoke first?"

"Sure!" Mort sneered. "You can smoke, but keep your hands high, or you'll die quick. Go ahead, have your smoke. I like standing here watching you. I like remembering that you're Rock Bannon and I'm Mort Harper and this is the last hand of the game and I'm holding all winning cards. I've got the girl and I've got the drop."

Carefully, Rock dug papers and tobacco from his breast pocket. Keeping his hands high and away from his guns, he rolled a cigarette.

"Like thinking about it, don't you, Harper? Killing me quick would have spoiled that. If you'd shot me while I was on the ground, it wouldn't have been good. I'd never have known what hit me. Now I do know. Tastes good, doesn't it, Mort?"

He dug for his matches and got them out. He struck one, and it flared up with a big burst. Rock smiled, and holding the match in his fingers, the cigarette between his lips, he grinned at Mort.

"Yes," he said, "it tastes good, doesn't it? And you've got the girl somewhere? Got her hid where I can't find her? Why, Mort, I'll have no trouble. I can read your mind. I can trail you anywhere. I could trail a buzzard flying over a snow field, Mort, so trailing you would be—" The match burned down to his fingers and he gestured with it, then as the flame touched them he let out a startled yelp and dropped the match, jerking his hand from the pain—the hand swept down and up, blasting fire!

Mort Harper, distracted by the gesture and the sudden yelp of pain, was just too late. The two guns boomed together, but Mort twisted with sudden shock, and he took a full step back, his face stricken.

Rock Bannon stepped carefully to one side for a better frontal target, and they both fired again. He felt something slug him and a leg buckled, and he fired again, then again. He shifted guns and fired a fifth shot. Harper was on his knees, his face white and twisted. Rock walked up to him and kicked the smoking gun from his hand.

"Where is she?" he demanded. "Tell me!"

Mort's hate filled face twisted. "Go to the devil!" he gasped hoarsely. "You go—to the devil!" He coughed, spitting blood. "Go to the devil!" he said again. Suddenly his mouth opened wide and he seemed gasping wildly for breath that he couldn't get; then he fell forward on his face, his fingers digging into the grass as blood stained the mossy earth beneath him.

Rock walked back to the horse and stood there, gripping the saddlehorn. He felt weak and sick, yet he didn't believe he had been hit hard. There was a dampness on his side, yet when he pulled off his shirt, he saw that only the skin was cut in a shallow groove along his side above the hip bone.

Digging stuff from his saddlebags, he patched the wound as well as he could. It was only then he thought of his leg.

There was nothing wrong with it, and then he saw the wrenched spur. The bullet had struck his spur, twisting and jerking his leg, but doing no harm.

Carefully, he reloaded his guns. Then he called loudly. There was no response. He called again, and there was no answering sound. Slowly, Rock began to circle, studying the ground. Harper had moved carefully through the grass, and had left little trail. Rock returned for his horse, and mounting, began to ride in slow circles.

Somewhere, Mort would have his horses, and the girl would not be far from them. From time to time he called.

Two hours passed. At times, he swung down and walked, leading the stallion. He worked his way through every grove, examined every boulder patch and clump of brush.

Bees hummed in the still, warm air. He walked on, his side smarting viciously, his feet heavy with walking in the high-heeled boots. Suddenly, sharply the stallion's head came up and he whinnied. Almost instantly, there was an answering call. Then Rock Bannon saw a horse, and swinging into the saddle he loped across the narrow glade toward the boulders.

The horse was there, and almost at once he saw Sharon. She was tied to the top of a boulder, out of sight from below except for a toe of her boot. He scrambled up and released her, then unfastened the handkerchief with which she had been gagged.

"Oh, Rock!" Her arms went about him, and for a long moment they sat there, and he held her close. After a long time she looked up. "When I heard your horse, I tried so hard to cry out that I almost strangled. Then when my mare whinnied, I knew you'd find us."

She came to with a start as he helped her down. "Rock! Where's Mort? He meant to kill you."

"He was born to fail," Rock said simply. "He was just a man who had big plans, but couldn't win out with anything. At the wrong time he was too filled with hate to even accomplish a satisfactory killin'."

Briefly, as she bathed her face and hands, he told her of what had happened at Poplar. "Your folks will all be back in their homes by now," he said. "You know, in some ways, Lamport was one of the best of the lot. He was a fighter—a regular bull. I hit him once with everything I had, every bit of strength and power and drive in me, and he only grunted."

They sat there in the grass, liking the shade of the white-trunked aspens.

"Dud and Mary are getting married, Rock," Sharon said suddenly.

He reddened slowly under the tan and tugged at a handful of grass. "Reckon," he said slowly, "that'll be two pairs of us!"

Sharon laughed gaily and turned. "Why, Rock! Are you asking me to marry you?"

"Nope," he said, grinning broadly. "I'm tellin' you! This here's one marriage that's goin' to start off right."

The steel-dust stallion stamped his hoofs restlessly. Things were being altogether too quiet. He wasn't used to it.